What's a R

Samantha Holt

Rogues of Redmere

Chapter One

C*ornwall, 1814*

"Bloody hurry up." The ship's captain peered down at Knight from the upper deck, moonlight highlighting his strained expression.

Knight merely grunted. Drake only wanted this done so he could be on his way with haste and return to Knight's sister. Knight grunted again. What his sister saw in Drake, he did not know, but she seemed happy to be his wife. He gripped the wooden crate tighter than he needed to. Didn't mean he had to be happy about her being married to a rogue.

Air whistled about them, tinged with the flavor of salt. The ping of metal on metal and the creak of wood drifted in with the breeze, punctuating an otherwise silent night. Stillness circulated the ship, the docks empty of the usual bustle of fishermen and the tide carefully nudging the ship from side to side, any power the waves possessed were lost when they entered the long harbor.

Above, an almost full moon gave them most of the light they needed, fingers of frosty light trickling over the fishing village and allowing them to douse the lanterns and ensure they could keep their nighttime activities secret. By day, they would appear legitimate businessmen. By night, and once across the sea to France, they were smugglers—corrupt to the core—the only sort of men able to access France during wartime with no questions asked.

An ominous shadow glided across the ship and Knight peered up to eye the cloud doggedly covering their only source of light. He sighed. Little had gone right tonight, and until the ship was safely abound for France, he could not relax.

"Are you going to help me with this damned thing or not?" demanded Nate, who clutched the other side of the crate.

Knight snorted. "I could lift all of these alone."

Nate arched a brow. Dark haired and wearing spectacles, Nate was well built, and though the glasses softened his looks, it made him no less handsome and aristocratic. He was not, however, as bulky as Knight. Nor as scarred. None of them were. Even Drake, who had been injured in battle and promptly forced to retire from the Navy could not match Knight's gruesome looks.

"If you want me to leave you to it..." Nate raised his hands and stepped away from the crate.

Air expelled from Knight's lungs as he was forced to take the weight of the crate. Most were stuffed with fabrics and were easy enough to carry. This one had to not only hold fabrics but also contained a person.

An *important* person.

A spy.

"Damn it, Nate." Knight struggled to move the crate across the deck.

Nate chuckled and came to take the weight on the other side once more. "Not so strong now, are you?"

Knight didn't respond. He only used his strength when necessary. After all, he'd done enough fighting in his life. That did not mean he was not tempted to wipe the smirk off Nate's face. The men he worked with were as close to friends as he'd ever had but they seemed to take great delight in riling him, knowing full well he wouldn't lay a hand on them.

Well, at least until Drake had started showing interest in Knight's sister. But after Drake had saved her life, Knight could hardly complain.

"Will you two cease gossiping like women and make haste?" Drake stepped down from the upper deck, his limp pronounced when he made his way down the steps. "We know the customs men are out. Louisa said they frequented the inn tonight. It's only a matter of time before they reach the docks."

Knight stiffened at the mention of Louisa. The owner of the Ship Inn had helped them many a time, and it was the place Knight frequented most. Sometimes he even stayed there if he had been drinking late. It had become something of a refuge—a place where no one cared what he did or with whom he spoke. Which, if it could be helped, he rarely did. Drake, in particular, was known for speaking without thinking and it got him into plenty of trouble. Knight would rather leave the conversing to him.

Especially when it came to Louisa. The beautiful innkeeper plagued his thoughts enough. He didn't need her softening to him.

"If you want us to move more quickly, why do you not come and give us a hand?" said Nate.

Drake folded his arms across his chest. "I captain this ship and I'm no ship hand. And, alas, my leg will not allow me to lift heavy objects."

Knight rolled his eyes. Drake's injury only caused him problems when he wished it.

"If you would stop complaining like an old woman, we would be done by now," Nate said through clenched teeth as they moved the final crate into place, the wood scratching across the surface of the oiled deck. He didn't envy the spy trapped inside the dark confines. Knight had done his duty to his country once before, and while they might be helping the cause, the lure of coin and an occupation had hooked him into helping the Earl of Redmere and his smuggling ring. He could certainly think of better things to do than sneak into the enemy's territory with little air and an uncomfortable journey ahead.

Knight peered across the harbor and hissed out a breath. "Hell fire." He pointed toward the hill that led down to the Cornish fishing village. Golden lights snaked down the slope at a pace, no doubt held by the excise men who patrolled the coasts in the hopes of catching smugglers in the act. Cornwall, in particular, was ideal for bringing goods in and out of France, especially wares that were no longer allowed thanks to the war. Unfortunately for them, it meant dodging those trying to catch them in the act was becoming harder.

"Damn it, must be customs men." Nate turned to Drake. "You make ready to leave. We'll distract them."

Knight shook his head. "I'll distract them. You'll ride home."

"But—"

Drake cut Nate off. "He's right. We cannot have the Earl of Redmere's brother caught with smugglers."

"They do not know you're smuggling anything," Nate protested.

"Leave the fighting to me," Knight said through clenched teeth.

The whole reason the earl had brought him on board was to be the aggressive face of the operation. With his bulk, height, and scar-riddled features, even he would be hard-pressed to think of a person better suited to heading up a smuggling operation. Not that it had been his life's ambition, but after his father disinherited him, and his time in the Army had all but crushed him, there were few options open to him. Hell, he'd fallen into lawless ways when Red had found him. The chances were he'd be dead or locked up if he'd continued down that path.

"Damn it, Knight." Nate's knuckles whitened as he balled a fist.

Drawing himself up to his full height, Knight glowered down at the man. Red would have his head if Knight let anything happen to his brother.

Nate's grin grew smug. "You do not scare me one jot, Knight."

Knight took a step forward, glancing briefly over his shoulder to eye the movement of the lanterns. Glimpses of glowing light highlighted the silhouettes of the ramshackle cottages that made up the bulk of the village. They only had a few minutes before the men were upon them.

"Nate," he growled.

Lifting his hands, Nate retreated a step. "Fine. Do as you will. Just do it with haste. They are almost upon us."

Drake directed the ship-hands to make ready. "I'll get her away. You go break some skulls or whatever is it you normally do," he told Knight.

Knight didn't respond. He avoided violence at all costs. His size attracted trouble as much as it prevented it, so sometimes it couldn't be prevented, but he'd do his damndest not to harm anyone. At least permanently. The last thing they needed was the attention of the government. Their work with the Crown was never officially sanctioned.

Dragging in his last breath of unhindered air, he pulled a wool scarf over his mouth and nose then yanked his cap down over his face. He didn't need the customs men recognizing him.

He slipped along the shadowy length of the harbor at pace, keeping his steps quiet. He smirked to himself. At least the Army had taught him one thing—how to move quietly for a man his size. There had been many a time his newfound skill had saved him from a bullet or a blade to the gut.

The excise men did not follow the same precautions. There were barked orders, the snort and whinny of horses, and the hollow stamp of hooves against the dry ground. Knight would know once they entered the cobbled length of the harbor.

Fishermen's boats creaked with the gentle tip of the waves entering the port. Beside him, the stone buildings in which the daily catch was unloaded provided protection from the moon every time she revealed herself from behind a cloud. He pressed deeper into the darkness and continued along until the clatter of horses was almost upon him.

Flatting his back to the stone wall, he waited, the jagged walls pressing into his shoulder blades. He curled his fingers around the hilt of his knife, the smooth wooden handle resting comfortably against his palm. Others preferred pistols for a quick response, but they took time to reload and were never accurate. Even if he wanted to spill blood tonight, shooting a man was never as easy as people assumed.

With any luck, he'd keep the ground clean tonight anyway. The men who patrolled the area were usually poorly paid and ill-trained. They should be easy to overcome.

His heart gave a thud in his ears at the change in sounds. The men had entered the main entranceway to the harbor where the carts were driven in to collect the catch. They moved with caution, given the restrained clatter against the flagstones.

Knight eased himself away from the wall long enough to catch sight of them. Three men, all on horseback. They'd made life harder for themselves by carrying lanterns. None would have quick access to their weapons. He allowed himself a small smile beneath the itchy wool. It would be even easier than he'd first thought.

Letting the shadows swallow him back up, he drew in measured breaths. Little scared him these days but it did not prevent the rush through his veins, the heavy thump in his ears. He tapped his knife once more, assuring himself it was there if necessary.

Launching forward, he grabbed the boot of the first man. A startled cry released from him, and he jerked against Knight's hold. The horse reacted to the sudden tug on the reins and bolted forward, leaving his passenger to flail and fall to the ground.

The two other men responded quickly, the grate of blades loosened from their scabbards making the flesh on Knight's arms prickle. Lanterns shattered to the ground, their brief light snuffed out on the cobbles.

A swift punch to the man's face rendered him senseless, allowing Knight to concentrate on the two men still in the saddle. He ducked a blade but felt the rush of air as it missed him by mere inches.

"Get him," bellowed the second man, his thin features briefly lit by the moonlight before it vanished under cloud cover.

Knight barreled toward him, launching himself high enough to wrap his arms about the man and drag him from the saddle. They fell together, Knight taking the brunt of the fall. Breath left his body, and his enemy's bony frame jabbed his ribs. Ignoring the pain that thudded along his spine, Knight rolled quickly, pinning the man beneath him. He spared the final rider a glance as the man turned his horse to make another run at Knight.

Turning his attention back to his captive, Knight wrapped his fingers about the man's neck while he squirmed beneath him. He felt the warm pulse of life under his fingertips and squeezed. The man clawed at his hands. Knight barely spared him a glance as he eyed the soldier on horseback, his gaze firmly on the drawn blade as the man descended upon him. Beneath him, the man went limp. Not dead, but he'd wake with a mighty headache.

Knight rolled as the blade swished over him. This time there wasn't even inches in it. The sword had caught his cap, dragging it off his head.

Coming to his feet, he curled his fists and faced the man as he made a third run. This would be his third and final, Knight would ensure that much. He waited until the man was nearly upon him before turning and sprinting toward the harbor edge, where stone gave way to sea. He twisted and faced the man again as the soldier was forced to bring his horse to a sudden halt.

Panic flared in the man's expression, and Knight used the opportunity to grab his arm, hauling him straight from the horse into the water. The resounding splash made Knight grin.

He peered into the inky darkness of the water. A head popped to the surface and flailed his arms.

"Help." His words were choked. "I cannot...swim..."

The man bobbed under. Knight closed his eyes briefly and drew in a long breath.

Damn it.

Divesting himself of his boots and jacket, he leaped into the sea. The cool shock of water pushed the air from his lungs. Knight swiped droplets from his face and swam over to where the man fought to stay afloat. He quickly grabbed the flailing man, barking an order to keep still that was muffled by the scarf across his lower face.

He dragged the man to the edge of the port and shoved him up onto the stone before heaving himself up. The soldier lay limp, but Knight could hear quietly frantic breaths from the man.

"Why...why did you not let me die?" the man whispered.

"I've seen enough blood," Knight muttered, coming to kneel over him. "But if you want to stay alive, you run from here and you do not come back. I might not be so generous next time."

Knight didn't wait for a response. He snatched up his cap and jacket and slipped his feet back into his boots, grimacing at every sodden movement. Retrieving the men's swords, he flung them into the ocean. The horses milled aimlessly about the port, but Knight knew they'd come to no harm. When discovered in the morning, the horses would be looked after by villagers until the three men were capable of riding them back to wherever they came from. As much as the local people disliked the customs men, who were not discrete in their enquiries and frequently threatened folk, they wouldn't risk drawing more attention to their small village.

Knight only hoped he had not done so either. It wasn't their first run in with the men, and so long as they continued smuggling, it would not be their last. Thankfully they were not alone in their attempts to get goods in and out of the country, and their operation was but a trifle compared to what some of the criminal element were partaking in.

The sea air sent a gust his way, wrapping it about his sodden clothes. He needed a warm bed and warmer whisky. He turned and headed in the direction of the inn.

Set atop the cliff that overlooked the rest of the village, lanterns shone their ambient light in warm greeting, having been responsible for many a man being lured to their drunken fates. It took plenty for Knight to get in such a state so no such fate awaited him tonight, but the pull of a comfortable bed and a place to hang his clothes was enough. He cut his way through the village, his movements slowed by his sodden clothes, then ascended the path up toward the ramshackle inn.

Little noises emanated from the building, but at this time of night he was not surprised. He pushed open the door to find a few patrons slumped across tables. It was not the best of inns nor the worst. One could be promised a clean bed and a hearty meal here, which was a lot better than many he had frequented. Louisa ran the pub with a tight hand and now that his sister worked here, their feminine touches could be seen. The floors were clean and the tables polished—at least the ones on which no one was slumped.

A fire crackled generously in the grate, and Knight made his way over, drawing off his boots and placing them in front of it. The bar was empty, but that didn't surprise him. At this time of night, Louisa and Julianna were likely abed. He used the opportunity to slip off his shirt and hang it over the fireguard. Shirtless, he ambled over to the bar and helped himself to a glass of whiskey.

"It's not raining."

Knight peered sideways. Louisa stood in the doorway of the kitchen, her golden hair in a frizzy halo about her face. Shadows lingered under her eyes. He looked away. Frizzy hair and dark eyes didn't prevent the clamp of desire in his gut.

She moved toward him, and he could swear he felt her gaze rake his half-naked body. His muscles tensed. There was no hiding the scars that riddled his back and abdomen. They were ugly and jagged and visible. He cared little for what anyone thought of his appearance.

Normally.

"Why are you so wet?" she asked, sliding onto the stool next to him and snatching the glass from his hand to refill it before shoving it back in his direction.

"I slipped."

"Slipped?" She let out a light laugh. "Well—"

The door to the inn swung open, bringing a fresh blast of frigid air. Knight straightened. This could not be good.

The Earl of Redmere strode straight over to him, removing his hat and shoving it under his arm. His gaze ran over Knight's sodden and unclothed state.

"Put some damned clothes on, Knight. I have news."

Chapter Two

Louisa shoved a loose strand of hair from her face and gave herself a mental shake. She'd seen men in various states of undress over the years—such came with the territory of being an innkeeper. It was not as though she had never seen a half-naked man before.

Knight strode over to the fireplace and snatched up his still sodden shirt, expression sour. Swallowing, Louisa grabbed a cloth and scrubbed furiously at a stain that had been etched into the bar long before she even married her late husband. No amount of scrubbing would remove it. But it was better than the alternative.

Staring at Knight.

She lifted her gaze and regretted it instantly. Heat flowed into her cheeks. She swung her gaze down again and concentrated on the circular stain. He was just a man. She dealt with them every day. Men of all varieties frequented her inn. Some were travelling through, some were locals. The customs men even drank here, and she'd played host to a few noble folk thanks to her private dining room and clean standards. The Ship Inn was no luxury accommodation and wherever there was alcohol, there was trouble, but she did her best with what she had to run a reputable place.

Knight and the Earl of Redmere both counted as nobles, but it was hard to think of either of them that way. She'd always known Red was above her station, but he never treated her as such, and thanks to her helping him out, hiding the occasional loot and warning them when customs men were about, they'd formed a beneficial friendship. In return for her aid, he kept her supplied with generous amounts of wine and anything else she might need.

As for Knight...well, it was still hard to believe he was a viscount. She had known little of him before his sister started working at the inn. On the run from her father and a vicious fiancé, Julianna had hidden out here and fallen in love with Drake, the captain of Red's ship. Thanks to Julianna, Louisa now knew a little more about Knight.

But only a little.

The great brute of a man remained as mysterious as he could. Even Julianna could not tell her much about the time between when Knight had been disowned by his father and his arrival in Cornwall. Lewis Knight had arrived in a flurry of fists with new scars across his face. That should have been all she needed to know about the man.

And yet...

She forced her gaze down while Knight fought to pull his soaked shirt over his head with a grumble.

Yet she could not help watching him. And wondering. How did he get all of those scars? There were several across his back—great big slashes and a handful of smaller ones to match the jagged one that cut across his eyebrow and the one beneath his lip. Another curved slightly across his chin. The one on his lip and eyebrow were instantly noticeable, both pale against his tanned skin. The one on his chin, however, was only obvious if a person studied him carefully. She was ashamed to admit that she had, far too many times.

The front door crashed open, and Louisa straightened. Few people visited the inn at this hour unless they had been travelling late. She'd already worked all day but one of her serving girls had fallen ill and Julianna was looking a little ashen so she had sent her to bed. When her husband sailed, Julianna stayed at the inn, declaring it far better than staying in their newly decorated, rather large house on the outskirts of the village alone.

So with no help, she'd rather hoped it would be a quiet night. By the looks of the four men, however, it did not appear her hopes would come true. They staggered in, crashing into one another and cutting an awkward path to the bar. One clutched what appeared to be an empty bottle. The fine cut of their clothing indicated they were visitors to the area with a little coin to spend.

Louisa drew up her shoulders and forced a cautious smile. So long as they behaved themselves, she was happy to take their coin. "What can I get you gentlemen?"

A lascivious smile curved the lips of the tallest man. He removed his hat and dropped it unceremoniously onto the bar. Beneath curly dark hair was a chiseled face that could put even the earl to shame. Eyes framed by generous lashes traveled over her person, making her skin prick. She kept her expression neutral.

"A little company would be nice," he drawled, his words softened by the alcohol that washed over her on his pungent breath.

The men with him snickered, and Louisa's smile dropped. "I serve alcohol and food only, gentlemen. If you seek company, I suggest you go into the village. If you're patient, the kitchen will be open in a few hours."

The tall man's gaze tracked over her once more, lingering on her chest. Though dressed modestly, there had never been any disguising her curves that too often got her into trouble. When she had first married and started working at the inn as a young woman, she'd been shocked by how her figure appealed to men. It was rare anyone made a comment these days, though. Most of her patrons respected her, and if they did not, they feared being cut off or barred.

The man leaned over the bar, both elbows resting on the wood. A light, clean scent broke through the air, slicing through the fragrances of hops and sea salt. It was quickly doused by the sour odor of alcohol as he smiled widely at her.

"I could make it worth your time." He reached for her.

Louisa stepped out of his reach and folded her arms. "You will not find what you are looking for here." She motioned to the door. "I think you should leave."

The man's expression darkened. His friends straightened. Louisa drew in a long breath and eyed the man coldly. He was not the first disrespectful man she had ever dealt with, but she really did not have the energy for a battle tonight.

The visitor glanced at his friends, and she saw his courage increase. For whatever reason, the man intended to make a show to his companions and her refusal of him had not helped matters. He moved around the bar quickly, forcing Louisa to back up against the corner of it. She held out both hands, and her palms met his chest but could not hold him back. He slammed himself up against her, jamming her back to the bar. A cry escaped her as the hard wood slammed into her spine.

"No one—" His words were cut off in a strangled cry as his body seemed to lift into the air, flew over the bar, and crashed onto a table with such force that the legs gave way and the whole piece of furniture crumbled to the floor.

Louisa blinked at Knight, not quite able to move. He stepped over to the man, towering way above him, and folded his arms. Red remained by the bar, utterly at ease. And why would he not be? Knight could take on all four of the men alone if he needed to.

"The lady said leave," Knight growled.

Louisa peeled herself away from the bar and brushed her hands down her apron. Her heart pressed hard against her breast bone, and she willed it to slow.

The man's companions eyed Knight, their gazes scanning his huge height, and as a group, hustled toward the door with little care for their fallen friend.

The tall man dragged himself from the floor with a groan and sent a scowl her way. "You'll—"

Knight snatched him by his collar before he could finish his sentence. "Leave," was all Knight said before flinging him out of the entrance and slamming the door shut behind all four men.

He edged over to the bar, and his gaze met hers cautiously. "Are you well?"

She sucked in a breath and nodded. "It was a fine job you were here."

"It was."

She peered at Red, who seemed to be suppressing a laugh. "What?"

Red grinned. "You forget I have seen you handle many a drunkard by the ear. Or by the balls when needs be."

"I had no desire to handle his balls." Louisa shuddered. For some reason, that man had truly frightened her. Probably because he was not just some silly drunk. He'd come here with a purpose and arrogance governed his behavior rather than alcohol.

"You should hire some protection," Knight muttered. "No job for a woman."

Louisa turned her attention fully to him and placed her hands to her hips. "Pardon?"

Knight's face reddened slightly. "I just mean—"

She lifted both brows. "I suppose I should go and work as a governess or something feminine like that."

Creases marred his forehead. "That's not what—"

"Louisa, can we use the private dining room? I have business I need to discuss with Knight," Red interrupted smoothly.

"Of course." She tilted her head and eyed Red. "Does Hannah know you are out at this hour?"

Red smiled. "Naturally. Do I ever do anything without my wife's say so these days?"

Louisa let her lips curve. The headstrong and intelligent woman had certainly done an outstanding job of taming the stubborn earl. Now that they were expecting their first baby,

Red had become an even more dedicated husband—if that was possible.

"Be sure to tell her I'm thinking of her in her confinement."

Red grimaced. "The sooner she is out of confinement, the better. I have had to invest in several hundred new books just to keep her occupied." He indicated to the private dining room. "Shall we?"

Knight grunted and followed Red. Louisa could not help eye those wide shoulders and the confident gait of Knight. She should not be watching him. Should certainly not be wondering about him. He made it clear that whatever had happened in his past—and even in his present—would remain secret. What was worse was she'd leapt from thinking about Red and Hannah's wonderful marriage to Knight's broad shoulders.

She shook her head to herself. Her marriage had been fine. One of practicality more than anything. She'd been an unexpected child to older parents of little wealth. Once they passed on, she would have had nothing. So when Jack offered for her hand, it seemed prudent to accept. She'd respected him as a man, and he had taught her everything she knew about running an inn, but there had been no passionate love between them.

A sigh escaped her, and she wished she could force it back in. It seemed as though everyone was getting married. Three men out of Red's main group were now wed. That only left Knight.

He would never marry, though, she was certain of that much. He didn't spend time with women—barely even acknowledged their existence. Heck, he hardly talked with those she considered his friends. Whether he thought of them as such, she did not know.

"You like him."

Louisa whirled. Julianna stood in the doorway leading from the accommodation to the bar. "Of course I don't," she protested. "I mean..." She trailed off, remembering with whom she was talking.

Julianna laughed. "I know my brother is not the most likeable of men, but I'm not wrong. I've seen you watch him."

Louisa forced a smile. "I watch everyone who enters my inn."

Julianna shrugged, her lips tilted. "I think you would work well together."

She shook her head frantically. "I work well alone." She cocked her head. "What are you doing up? I told you to go to bed."

"I slept for a while but it was fitful. I decided I might as well come and aid you."

Louisa peered at her friend. That slight ashen cast had faded but there was something different about her. She hoped Julianna was not sickening. Since her arrival at Penshallow, she had been a wonderful help and had become a close friend—one of the few Louisa had. She hardly had time for friendships. And she certainly did not have time for relationships. She liked her life as it was. Simple, routine, and productive. Men only complicated life.

Especially a man like Knight. Underneath that brooding exterior had to be complications. She'd wager her inn on that.

Hinges squeaked, and the fire spitting in the grate announced a new arrival. Louisa stiffened. Hopefully those men were not foolish enough to return. She eased her grip on the cloth in her hand when a lone man stepped in. With any luck, they would have no more commotion for the evening.

The newcomer strode over to the bar and offered a genial smile. "Are you by any chance Mrs. Carter?"

"Who wants to know?"

He slipped onto the stool in front of the bar and removed his hat, rifling a hand through his hair. "I'm Ralph Carter." He chuckled as she blinked at him. "Your stepson."

Chapter Three

"How did tonight go?" Red dropped onto a chair and leaned back to eye Knight. The earl, dressed casually, but as usual impeccably, affected his typical insouciant air.

Knight shut the door to the dining room behind him. Small but clean and with welcoming flames crackling in the petite fireplace, the private dining room usually played host to noble folk or those with a little extra coin, but the four of them—Red, Nate, Drake and himself—sometimes used it for conversations that should not be overheard.

Knight shrugged and strode over to the fire. His clothes remained uncomfortably plastered against his skin, and he needed a moment to swipe away the image of that bastard touching Louisa. He peered into the dancing flames. That woman was starting to occupy his thoughts far too often.

"Considering your appearance, I take it all did not go smoothly?"

Knight glanced sideways at Red. The earl was the money and the brains behind their operation. When Nate had been unable to join the military thanks to his need for glasses, his older brother had taken it upon himself to ensure Nate could fulfill an element of helping his country. It was an unusual way to help for sure, but it worked for them all. It put Knight's brawn to effective use and earned good money. For he and Drake, who had both been close to penniless and utterly aimless before meeting Red, it had likely saved their lives.

Not that Knight would ever tell the earl that. The man was arrogant enough as it was.

"I handled it," muttered Knight.

"And went for a swim?" Red motioned to the chair opposite.

Knight ignored the invite. "Customs men were about tonight. I...incapacitated them." He turned his attention back to the fire, allowing his focus to soften until the flames became a giant orange blur while he rested one arm against the cold, uneven stone walls of the building. What happened tonight was not a common occurrence. They were usually able to evade the customs men but his clash with them would draw more attention to Penshallow.

There was little else he could have done, however, and Knight could not claim to feel much of anything about the clash. The men were alive and would be sore and likely a little chastened, but he had a job to do just as they did.

With any luck, thanks to the prevalence of smuggling in Cornwall, the undermanned excise troops would not have the ability to increase their presence locally and things could continue as normal.

"Knight."

Knight turned to face Red. The man motioned to the seat opposite. Reluctantly, he eased himself onto the wooden chair that felt too spindly for his large body. Since he turned fourteen, he'd been too large for everything. Too large for women, too large to be a gentleman, too large for anyone to see him as anything other than a brute.

He huffed to himself. Well, that suited him just fine.

He peered at Red. Though the earl did not always involve himself in the physical work, the man was strong with the elegant looks of someone brought up on money. Red never treated Knight as anything other than a fellow man, even prior to discovering Knight had noble blood in him, but Knight always felt like a beast next to the perfectly polished man. He supposed Red had not always been quite so polished, but marrying had created a calmness about him. Gone were the days of nursing a whisky until the early hours.

Which begged the question, why was Red here at this hour?

Knight eyed the scarred tabletop, running a ragged fingernail down one of the grooves. He was not sure he wanted to know. Whatever it was, it could not be good news. This was why he avoided being anything other than the physical face of things. He loathed sitting and discussing things. If it could not be solved with his hands, he didn't want to know.

"All is well," he assured Red. "No one saw anything but me and none would be able to recognize me."

Red nodded. "I know you can handle things." He leaned forward. "But I did not come here to discuss our business arrangements."

Knight scowled. "What is it?"

Rubbing a hand across his face, Red took a lengthy inhale and met Knight's gaze. "I received word that your father has passed."

Knight stared at Red and waited for some kind of emotion to wash over him. A thud of his heart perhaps. The sick feeling in his stomach. None of it came. His father had been a heartless bastard and had beat any feeling out of him long ago. Still, he'd imagined this day and had expected some sort of emotion about it, maybe triumph even. Instead, it had left him cold. It seemed the years in the Army and the time after that had ensured he would never truly feel anything ever again.

Moments passed, the crackle of the fire and the occasional sound of footsteps from the taproom punctuating the silence. Aware of Red watching and waiting for a reaction, Knight stood quickly, the chair screeching in protest against the floor as he pushed it back. He strode back over to the fire and shoved his hands in his pockets.

Red rose from the table and came to stand at Knight's side. He leaned a shoulder against the wall as though he had all the time in the world.

"After what he did to Julianna, he deserves death," Knight muttered.

Red made no comment. If he thought the statement unfair, he made no sign of it. As far as Knight was concerned, trying to force his sister into marriage to a man who was known for killing and harming his wives, had been the worst of all his misdeeds. Whatever his father had done to him was inconsequential. He could handle it all. Julianna was an innocent, though, and never deserved to be forced to run from her home and have her life put in danger.

"Does she know yet?" Knight rotated to view Red.

He shook his head. "I was going to leave it to you to tell her."

"How did you find out?" No one knew of Knight's presence in Cornwall.

"A letter from the estate asking after your sister. I thought after what happened previously, it would be prudent to speak with you before giving out any information."

Knight nodded. There was no one left to harm his sister after the man who had wanted to marry her tried to kidnap her and was put on trial, but with Knight's activities, it was safer to keep her whereabouts quiet. He did not want anyone ever using her against him. However, it seemed rumor of her location had spread.

"They are looking for the heir to the title." Red pulled a letter out from the inside of his jacket and handed it over.

Knight ran a finger over the broken wax seal—the initials of his father stamped into it. Exhaling, he opened the letter and scanned the hastily scrawled contents. Knight shook his head. "All that will be left is an empty house and a penniless title." He could not keep the bitterness from his voice.

Until his father had disinherited him, he'd indulged grand ideas of being the sort of viscount his father's estate deserved. But his father had plundered and pillaged their lands to feed his greed, selling off whatever land he could, neglecting tenants' houses and the farms, and racking up great debts so he could live the sort of lifestyle he thought he deserved.

Now all that was left was debt and a title. Whatever else his father had owned would have been willed on to others, Knight was certain of that. Knight would have to do what he could with the entailed lands to cover the death duties and debts against the estate. Anything that could be sold off would be, and he'd have to find a tenant for the house with haste.

"You should go home. Settle the debts," Red advised.

"I'd rather die than set foot in that place again," Knight muttered.

"There's nothing to do for a while here, and if you do not, they shall come looking for you."

Knight nodded. He knew he could not avoid returning home really, but he'd be damned if he'd go eagerly.

"Take my carriage," Red offered. "That way you will be back by the time Drake has returned from France."

Knight bunched a hand at the thought of riding in Red's crest-emblazoned town coach, crunching the letter between his palm and fingers. Noble blood might run through his veins, but he didn't belong in such a vehicle—he knew that much. Too many years had passed, and he'd seen too much. He was as rough as the next man and had no business arriving at a grand estate in such finery.

Even if it was now his estate.

God, the sooner it was gone, the better. He nodded. He'd take the damned coach if it meant he could have everything settled and return to Cornwall promptly. If he didn't, he would be relying on mail coaches for most of the journey to Northumberland. While they were fast, he'd have to hop from coach to coach, eating up more time than he wished to spend on this matter.

Red patted Knight's shoulder. "I'll have the coach ready by mid-morning. You had better get some rest before the journey."

Knight waved away the suggestion. He'd learned to go without sleep when needed and could rest on the journey. His time in the Army had taught him to snatch rest when and where he could, which meant he could sleep practically anywhere.

"I had better tell Julianna." Knight glanced at the crumpled letter. If only Drake were here. He'd be better at comforting Julianna. As much as Knight loved her, he had little idea what to do with his much younger sister after so many years apart.

"Louisa will comfort her."

He lifted his gaze to Red's. How the hell did he know what he was thinking?

Red's lips curved. "You are more obvious than you realize, Knight. Perhaps you are getting soft in your old age."

"Not likely."

"I shall leave you to it and arrange for the carriage to be made ready. Hannah will be wanting to know why I rushed out so quickly too." Red exited the dining room, leaving the door slightly ajar.

Knight caught sight of Julianna talking to Louisa and a patron he did not recognize. There would be no putting it off until morning either then. He'd have to tell his sister now. Eyeing the letter once more, he crumpled it up and threw it in the fire, watching with satisfaction as the wax seal melted into oblivion.

The sooner this was dealt with the better—for both of them. And then he could return to this life. The life he was meant for. The life of a smuggler.

Chapter Four

Opening her mouth then closing it, Louisa studied the man in front of her. He was no rich man, but he had a charming air about him. His clothes were rumpled and a little threadbare but clean, and his accent was lilted—almost Northern—though she supposed time living elsewhere could have done that. He was about the same age as her—eight and twenty or so. Around the age Ralph Carter would have been had he still been alive.

Which he was not.

"Ralph is dead," Louisa blurted out.

He smiled and chuckled. "As you can see, I am not."

She shook her head rapidly and tightened her grip on the cloth in her hand. Ralph had been presumed killed during the early years of the war a few months before she had married her husband. She'd never even met him. But Jack had grieved for the young man, and there had been no word otherwise.

"You cannot be," she whispered, aware of Julianna hovering nearby, concern etched onto her brow.

The man smiled sheepishly. "I know this might come as a shock. I'm only sorry I could not return before my father passed."

Louisa felt her chin quiver and tightened her jaw. "You are many, many years too late for that."

Something flickered in the man's eyes, but he quickly buried it. "I regret that," he said, his voice hollow.

Scanning his features, she looked for some sign of Jack. They had the same coloring—or at least similar. Jack's eyes had been darker, but she knew her husband had chestnut hair in his younger years. This man's was chestnut with a hint of red.

Swallowing, Louisa lifted her chin. "Why did you not get in touch? Let your father know you were alive?"

He gave a regretful smile. "I was not aware he thought me dead until it was too late. There was an error, and my death was incorrectly reported. By the time I found out what had happened, he had died. It did not seem worth returning home." He shrugged.

Fingers to either side of her head, she attempted to rub away the burgeoning headache. "Where have you been all this time?"

"Bristol. I worked at a sawmill."

Louisa glanced around. No one here would know who Ralph was or even recognize him but perhaps some of the older members of the village would. She noticed Red lingering casually at the end of the bar, having given up on leaving for home, perhaps because of what he'd overheard. She sent a questioning look his way, but he shrugged. Red had no idea if this was really Ralph or not.

She sighed. If he was, she had a duty to Jack's memory to ensure he was well. "Can...can I get you a drink? You must have had a long journey."

"An ale would be nice." His smile expanded. "I can see why my father married you."

"You could have come and visited before," she said stiffly as she grabbed a mug and filled it before putting it in front of him. "What brings you home now?"

He hesitated a moment, opening his mouth then closing it before meeting her gaze. "I'm here to claim my inheritance, of course."

Cold dread rolled over her, pooling in her stomach. She stared at him. Surely he could not mean...?

"Pardon?" The word came out a whisper.

"I've decided it's time to return home and claim my inheritance." Ralph took a lengthy gulp of ale and wiped his mouth with the back of a hand, resting an arm on the bar. "By that, I mean the inn."

Behind her, Julianna gasped. Louisa could not even do the same. All the air vanished from her lungs.

"No." She spoke before she'd managed to register a thought. No. He could not have the inn. She'd worked hard her whole adult life to ensure the roof over her head and income remained secure.

"The inn only passed to you as my father had no surviving heirs. At least that was what everyone thought."

Louisa met his gaze, saw the slight amusement creasing his eyes. Indignation made her cheeks hot. How could he find this entertaining? He was talking about taking her livelihood away.

"No," she repeated, with more strength this time.

"You do not have much choice in the matter. The law of the land would agree with me. I am my father's sole heir so this inn belongs to me." He jabbed a finger against the wooden bar.

Fixing him with a cold glare, Louisa folded her arms across her chest and willed her pulse to slow. "I do not even know if you are Ralph Carter. You could be anyone."

"I have documents that can prove I am him." He pulled out a crumpled letter and spread it out on the bar. Even after all of these years, she recognized Jack's handwriting.

"But—"

"I also have the deeds to this inn, but I like to keep this letter close. Seeing as it's from my father." His smile thinned as though weighted by the threat she saw flicking in his gaze.

Red must have sensed this too as he moved closer and gave her a small nod, letting her know he was around if she needed aid.

"You cannot just expect..." She inhaled. "What do you expect me to do? Hand over the inn to you?"

Ralph smirked. "My father married a smart woman it seems."

"You must be mad. I will do no such thing."

She watched him drain the ale, fists curled at her sides. His Adam's apple bobbed while he drained the last drops. She had to resist the desire to shove him back or swing a punch at him. Every part of her felt hot and prickly. Her limbs were shaky. It had taken years to prove herself as capable of running the inn and even longer to make it reasonably profitable. What sort of a man walked in and laid claim to a place he had not set foot in for a decade?

Ralph placed the mug down with a flourish and rose from the stool. "I will give you two weeks, Mrs. Carter."

"Two weeks?" she echoed.

"Two weeks to make arrangements to leave. Or else I shall have you thrown out."

Red stood, his jaw clenched. Louisa was half-tempted to have the earl throw Ralph bodily out and see how he felt about it, but it would not help her cause. Julianna moved closer, coming to Louisa's side.

"You cannot take my inn from me!" Louisa cried.

"You certainly cannot," Julianna agreed.

"Two weeks." He donned his hat and pushed a coin across the bar. "Thank you for the ale. I shall be seeing you soon, Stepmother."

Louisa watched the man leave, forcing herself to draw deep breaths through her nostrils until he had left. She collapsed against the bar, digging both palms into the scarred wood.

"He cannot do such a thing, surely?" Julianna asked, looking to Red.

Red lifted his shoulders. "If he is Ralph Carter, he is heir to the inn." He shook his head. "Are you certain it is him?"

"The letter he showed me was from his father. How else would he have it?" Louisa dropped her head onto her arms and sighed. "What can I even do?"

Julianna rubbed a soothing hand up and down her back. "We will think of something."

"You need to check he is who he says he is. It is strange, him returning home after so long," Red mused. "I shall make a few enquiries on your behalf."

Louisa lifted her head. "You would do that for me?"

Red grinned. "Naturally. After all, you have helped me and my men out many a time. I believe we likely owe you one. But you should make your own enquiries. Where did he say he had been this whole time?"

"Bristol. He mentioned something about working at a mill." Louisa straightened. Perhaps with Red's help, she would not lose the inn after all. Red was right. Ralph's sudden return was strange, and from what she knew of him from Jack, he would never do such a thing to family. Admittedly, years could change a person, but so drastically?

Unfortunately, she did not have long to find out if her suspicions were correct.

"I have a suggestion." There was a slight hint of a smile touching to corners of Red's mouth that made Louisa frown.

She peered at him. "Yes?"

"Go to Bristol. Find out what you can," Red insisted. "I have been around enough dishonest men to sense when something is not right. I would go for you but you know I cannot leave Hannah."

Louisa straightened and smoothed her hair back from her face. "And I cannot leave the inn. Not for so long. I do not even know how long it will take me to get to Bristol." Given she had never left Cornwall, she was not even certain where it was. Upwards was about as much as she knew because any other direction would lead her to the sea.

"About three days by mail coach. But you can take my coach," Red suggested. "It will be a lot quicker and you'll be there in two."

Julianna nodded. "And I can look after things while you are gone."

Louisa glanced between her two friends. Since inheriting the inn, she could not remember a day when she had been anywhere else. She occasionally went to Truro or some of the nearer towns to negotiate with suppliers but the thought of leaving the inn, knowing that predatory man was waiting in the eaves to swoop in and steal her life's work, made her gut clench.

She chewed on her bottom lip as she weighed the options. "That is still at least four days. If not more. I shall need time to investigate." But she could not just sit back and let Red do all the work and simply wait for the inn to be taken from her.

Red motioned to Julianna. "Julianna is more than capable."

Louisa nodded slowly. She was. Julianna had breeding and an education that Louisa did not, yet she proved herself the hardest worker Louisa had ever had and could be mightily fierce when needed. She swung her gaze to Julianna. "Are you certain you can manage?"

"Of course." The pretty, dark-haired woman nodded firmly. "We cannot let him take the inn, Louisa. This place would not be the same without you."

How could she argue with that? She had to know for certain if this man was really Ralph, and as much as the earl had contacts and investigators at his disposal, the quickest way to establish who he was, would be to go to where he'd been living for so long.

"Very well. I shall do it."

Chapter Five

Crisp, salt-ripened air blew across the cliff tops, riffling Knight's hair. He put on his hat and strode out to meet the coach as it drew to a halt outside the inn. Gleaming under the early morning sun that peeked through scattered clouds, the carriage was drawn by four mottled gray horses. Knight huffed out a breath. He'd feel a damned fraud arriving home in such a thing.

Behind him, the inn door slammed shut, pushed into its resting place by a sudden gust of wind. It was likely Julianna seeing him off. After he'd informed her of their father's death, he'd spent the night nursing a drink, and she'd busied herself with work. Neither of them had it in them to mourn the man. He turned.

"Knight?"

His name on her lips curled around his insides, tying tight. What the devil was she doing here?

Louisa peered at the bag he clutched in one hand. His belongings were sparse, but he'd gathered up what he needed early this morning, including a change of clothes and his spare pistol. Travelling in such grandeur could attract attention, and he'd be damned if he would not be prepared.

It took him a moment to notice she too clutched a travelling bag. He'd found himself distracted by the way the cool air made her cheeks pink and whisked tiny fair curls around her face. She wore a simple pale brown spencer that drew his attention inevitably down to the curves beneath that were carefully hugged by a simple column of linen.

She shifted, curling both hands around the worn leather handle of her bag. "Are you going somewhere?"

He shifted his attention back to her face. "Yes."

"In the earl's coach?"

"Yes."

She bit down on her bottom lip and shook her head. "As am I."

He lifted a brow. "The earl offered me his coach to travel to Northumberland."

Her lips tilted. "And he offered it to me to travel to Bristol. It seems Red has been generous indeed with his transport."

Knight cursed under his breath. Damn that man. What was he thinking? Red knew Knight would not want company for this journey. Especially from Louisa. As much as he'd like to think he had given nothing of his interest in her away, Red was no fool. The bloody man had come up with this ploy to ensure they spent time together.

Well, the man might not be a fool but he was an idiot if he thought time together would do anything. Louisa had no interest in him and rightly so. What could a man like him ever give a woman like her?

"I have to go with haste." Knight handed his luggage over to the footman.

Louisa scowled and took several steps forward, thrusting out her travelling bag to the man while his back was turned. Before the footman could return to take it, Knight snatched it from her and deposited it back on the doorstep of the inn.

"What do you think you are doing?" She trailed after him and seized the bag, stomping back over to the carriage.

Knight went to grab the bag again, but she slapped his hand away.

He eyed her, brows lifted. Louisa had a fierce temper when necessary but it was rarely directed at him. "You can go another time. My business is urgent."

And he could not travel with her. He just could not.

"As is mine!"

"You can go to Bristol on a different day. Or catch a mail coach."

Her eyes flared. "Red promised his coach to me. *You* can take a mail coach if travelling with me is so terrible."

He grimaced. The last thing he wanted to do was insult her, but the thought of being in such close confines with this woman made the knot in his gut tie tighter. Better to have her angry with him than have to suffer the torture of being so close to her and not being able to do a thing about it.

"I need to get to Northumberland," he explained gruffly.

"Is this something to do with Julianna?"

"In a way."

Her defiant posture softened, as he knew it would. His sister and Louisa were as close as siblings themselves. If she thought Julianna was in danger once more, she would let him go without a fight, surely?

She pursed her lips, drawing his attention to them. There'd been too many times he'd thought about those lips and wondered at their softness and taste. Wondered if any man was ever lucky enough to feel them against his skin. As far as he knew, Louisa had no time for lovers—for which he was grateful—even though he tortured himself with those thoughts out of habit. He smirked to himself. When had he ever done any different? He deserved a lifetime of torment for his sins, as far as he was concerned.

"Well, then," she said gently, lowering the bag from the defensive position in front of her.

Knight released a long breath. He let his shoulders soften. But before he could say anything, she shoved past him, threw her bag at the unsuspecting footman who fumbled to catch it, and flew up the steps into the coach.

Opening his mouth, then shutting it, he straightened once more. He should have known Louisa would not give up without a fight. He thrust his head through the carriage door to see her settled against the plush velvet seats. She smoothed down her skirt then offered him a serene smile.

"Bristol is on your way and will not add to your journey," she said reasonably.

Knight gripped the doorframe until the wood bit into his palms. What was he going to do? Haul her back to the inn over his shoulder? He could if he really wanted. It would be easy. Despite her inner strength and her ability to throw the occasional punch when bar fights broke out, she was no match for him. She'd weigh little more than a grain of sand to him.

Jaw clenched, he glanced over her. She met his gaze, unblinking. He eased his grip on the doorframe and grunted. "Fine."

Her smile expanded, satisfaction lighting her expression. She quickly quashed it and turned her gaze to her hands that she twined in her lap. He stepped away to give instructions to the driver then climbed into the carriage, his weight making it rock as he settled onto the seat opposite her.

Though it was not the first time he'd travelled in the earl's carriage, he had never done it alone. The interior was fragranced with delicate flowers that had been placed in holders by each door and small cushions trimmed with some sort of intricate pattern that his sister could probably name were propped on each seat in matching dark blue fabric. Curling a lip, he took one and shoved it aside to enable himself to settle properly onto the seat.

Setting his gaze on the inn outside, he watched it vanish into the distance as the driver followed the road that led over the cliff tops and toward the next town. He stole the briefest of glances at Louisa when he noted her fingers tugging at the ribbon that dangled from her bonnet down to her lap. Regret itched his gut.

Louisa never left the inn. Ever. In his years here, she and the inn had been one and the same. Everyone knew the tavern was practically her lifeblood. If he was a better man, he'd reach over and take her hand or say something comforting. Whatever reason she was going to Bristol, she was going reluctantly.

Perhaps it had been about whatever Julianna was going to tell him. He'd forgotten she'd tried to tell him something before he'd interrupted with the news of their father.

The scent of the flowers mingled with the clean fragrance of Louisa—a soapy aroma that he'd recognize anywhere. He blew out a breath and shoved open one of the windows, allowing in an aggressive gust of wind. Curls ruffled around Louisa's face and he exhaled again, slamming the window shut. He'd have to suffer or else she'd freeze.

"It will be about two days to Bristol. The driver knows of a place to stop and rest the horses."

She nodded, attention fixed on the ribbon she'd looped around one finger. Several beats of silence passed. Normally, he loved silence. Sleeping on the streets or in busy inns, even out in the countryside while battle roared on around him had made him appreciate every moment of quietness. But not today. He did not like Louisa's silence one bit. What was so urgent in Bristol that it was doing this to her?

He shook his head to himself. If he were Drake or Nate, or even Red on occasion, he'd be charming her in an instant. But he was not like any of them. His rough life meant little time for women, and they avoided him anyway.

"Why do you need to go home?" she blurted out.

He was surprised Julianna had not mentioned anything to her but it was clear Louisa had her own problems. He frowned to himself. Or else his sister knew of Red's plan for them to travel together and had deliberately concealed the details of their separate journeys.

"My father died."

Her mouth formed a silent 'oh.' She unfurled the ribbon from her finger. "I am sorry." Creases appeared between her brows. "At least, I..." She trailed off and glanced at his hand.

He looked down and realized his knuckles were white from his clenched fist. He released it.

"After what he did to Julianna, I cannot grieve for that man."

"Is Julianna well? She did not mention anything to me."

He shrugged. "I do not think she grieves for him anymore than I do."

Louisa tucked her bottom lip under her teeth briefly. "Grief is a funny thing, though."

Knight would not tell her he knew grief all too well. That there were men out there he felt a lot more for than his father. Whose deaths deserved grief.

"So you are returning home for his funeral?" she pressed.

Not if he could help it. He was not sure if any arrangements had been made, but he would do what he must and leave as soon as humanly possible.

"I am going to settle his debts."

"Oh." A hand went to her mouth. "You are a viscount now!"

He snorted. The title meant little, especially now it had been tarnished by his father's actions. Decades of legacy were gone, and as far as he was concerned, he had little duty to it—his father made sure he was aware of how unqualified he was to be a titled gentleman. He had to agree now. He was no more suited to the life of a gentleman than Drake was to a life on land.

"I am a penniless viscount. It means little." He eyed the passing countryside, empty save from the occasional sorry-looking tree and gray boulders lumped in piles from one of the many abandoned copper mines.

"So I do not need to call you 'my lord?'" she teased.

He gave her a look. The last time he'd been addressed as that had been the day he'd left home, when his valet had packed up his belongings and expressed sorrow at his being thrown out. These days he was about as far from a lord as a man could get.

"I suppose not." She smiled. "I hear Northumberland is beautiful, though. It might be nice to return home."

"It is beautiful," he admitted.

And it was one of the reasons Cornwall had appealed to him. They were both home to that wild sort of rugged beauty that a man could get lost in. There were no huge, bustling cities, filled with smog and dirt and noise.

It would not be 'nice' to return home, however. He had no idea what sort of greeting he could expect after more than a decade away, and he dreaded to think what state the estate had been left in. He'd be lucky to return to more than a ruin.

"Why the need to go to Bristol?" he asked before she could question him more about his estate and family. "You do not have family there, do you?"

She shook her head. "I have no family. Well, at least I do not think I do. A man arrived in Penshallow last night, claiming to be Jack's son."

"He's dead."

Louisa nodded. "He says the news of his death was a mistake and that he was not harmed but had been living and working in Bristol for some time."

Knight rubbed a hand across his stubbled jaw. "The Army is known to report men missing when it's simply a clerical error. Such is the mess of war."

She narrowed her gaze at him. "You know from experience?"

He ignored the question. Few knew of his time in the war. Even Red had the bare minimum. Well aware of the rumor circulating about his history, he was happy to keep it that way. If folk thought him a terrifying criminal on the run or the son of a famed pirate, so be it, and it forced them to keep their distance, he was more than happy for those rumors to persist.

"You do not believe he is who he claims he is?" he asked.

She wrapped her arms about her waist. "He wants the inn, Knight."

"Like hell." The words came out hard and forceful, like a punch landing just so.

Louisa chuckled. "I almost said as much."

"Your stepson has returned and wants your inn?" he clarified.

"Indeed."

"But you do not think he is your stepson?"

She gave a rueful smile. "It could be wishful thinking. However, it was odd, his sudden return. He said he learned of his father's death and had decided there was no sense in coming home previously. From what little I knew of Ralph, that does not sound like him. Jack had many letters from him, and he'd been a dedicated son and happy at the news of our engagement. I know because I had to go through them all after Jack died."

Knight had to look away and fix his gaze unseeingly on the countryside. The thought of Louisa having to deal with the death of a husband and the running of an inn alone at a young age created uncomfortable sensations in his chest. Sensations he did not wish to linger over.

"Did he have proof that he is Ralph?" he queried.

She pursed her lips. "He had a letter from his father, and said he had more evidence at his lodgings."

"A letter does not mean much."

"He has the deeds too. Or so he claims. I cannot help but think if he has returned to claim the inn as his, he must have enough to ensure his claim cannot be questioned." She sighed.

"Or he could be taking a gamble that you would not fight him on it."

Her gaze shot to his and that helplessness faded, replaced with the fire of determination. God help him, it made him want to lean forward and drag her into his arms and kiss her until she was warm and supple and had forgotten every worry.

"I will fight him on this. I intend to find out who he is for certain."

Knight nodded. "Good."

"He says I have two weeks," she muttered.

"Two weeks?"

"To leave—"

Her words were cut off as the carriage slammed to a sudden halt, flinging her forward. Knight instinctively grabbed her, his body taking the brunt of her fall. She flattened her palms against his chest and looked up at him. Every muscle in his body tensed. The air in the carriage grew weighted, making him feel as though he waded through water just to make his next movement.

Shouts from outside snapped his attention away. He cursed under his breath and pushed Louisa back. "Stay here." Reaching for the pistol on his belt, he hastily loaded it, cognizant of Louisa's wide-eyed stare. He pressed his face to the side of the carriage and peered out. Just as he'd thought.

"Highwaymen," he muttered.

Chapter Six

"But—"

Knight was gone before Louisa could utter another word. He slipped out of the door with surprising stealth for a man of his size. Pressing her head against the side of the carriage like Knight had, she could view the two men in front of the vehicle, presumably making their demands. Her mouth dried, and she had to force herself to swallow.

Where was Knight? Oh Lord, they were all going to end up dead. She could not see him at all. He must have slipped around the carriage somehow.

None of the highwaymen were on horseback and the carriage was manned by two footmen and a driver, so they outnumbered their attackers, but these men carried weapons. One had a pistol while the others had blades.

The driver possessed a gun surely? And Knight had his pistol. Cornwall was known for its dangerous roads thanks to its barren stretches of land, and with plenty of places to hide from any kind of retaliation, holding up travelers was an effortless way to make profit.

They would be sorely disappointed with her lack of riches, however. And disappointed highwaymen were dangerous.

One of the men lifted the pistol up to the driver. A squeak escaped her, and she pressed a hand to her mouth. She leaned farther forward to get a better view and spied Knight coming up from the side, his pistol drawn and pointed at the gunman. Louisa allowed herself a slow, shaky breath. Knight had likely dealt with many a crook. He would have no trouble handling these men.

A hand thrust through the window and a cry escaped her as she darted back, grubby fingers almost snatching a fistful of hair. She scrabbled back on the chair when the door flew open and a face thrust in the door. His gapped smile mocked her, and he lifted a sizeable knife, motioning with it.

"This way, if you will, my lady."

She glanced around the confines of the cabin. There was no escape, and she could not tell what was happening outside any longer. She slid herself off the seat, gaze set on the blade that the man taunted her with.

Moving slowly, she climbed out of the carriage, hands raised. She forced her body to stiffen in an attempt to cover how her limbs shook. The man grabbed her, constraining her against his body with an arm banded about her waist. The knife glinted menacingly by her face.

"Step back," the man holding her ordered Knight.

Knight's gaze met hers, and she frowned. She saw no defeat in his eyes, no frustration. Coolly, he took a pace back and lowered the pistol he had pointed at the other man. Louisa quickly took in the situation, pushing herself to calmly calculate what was happening—just like she would were it a fight at the inn or some other fracas. The man with the pistol kept it centered on the driver. The two footmen had their hands raised and were near the second man who watched them.

And the third man had his blade dancing close to her cheek. She drew in a shuddery breath. One wrong move and he could slice her with ease. If she could only figure out how to get away from that knife. If she threw herself down to the floor, that might do it, but it was a risk.

She met Knight's gaze again, and he gave her an almost imperceptible nod. She scowled. Surely he could not understand what she was thinking? She implored him with her gaze to give her another sign of some sort but he'd turned his attention back to the lead man.

"All you need to do is give us yer coin, and we'll leave yer be." The gunman jerked his gun at the driver. "Tell yer driver to get down and we can get this over with."

Knight nodded. "Johnson, will you come down, if you please?" Knight glanced back at Louisa and mouthed something.

She realized, as she threw herself hard to the ground, it was *now*.

A shot rang out. She lifted her head to see the man who'd been holding her clutching his arm as he staggered back. Blood seeped from between his fingers and he dropped onto his rear, his face ashen. The blade fell from his grip and clattered onto a rock. Louisa scrabbled forward to grab it and peered around at Knight while she clutched the handle of the weapon in both hands in an attempt to stop it shaking.

Before the gunman let off a shot, Knight raced forward and used his brute strength to drive the man to the ground. He was weaponless within moments and knocked senseless with two punches. The third man dove forward, his weapon thrust out.

"Knight," she cried out in warning, but too late. As Knight swung around, the blade tore through his clothes. Knight's face contorted, and he swung a fist at the man, propelling it into his gut. The man collapsed and gasped and flailed like a fish out of water. Knight finished him off with a quick kick to the head and his eyes rolled back.

It happened so quickly, Louisa hardly had time to process it. She remained crouched on the ground, her grip on the blade handle so tight that her fingers started to tingle. Knight strode over, a hand held out, but her arms were stiff and her legs felt like liquid.

"You are safe now," Knight said.

It was all she needed to hear, somehow. She let the knife drop from her aching fingers and took his hand. The warm, callused touch eased through her body, enabling her to come to her feet and draw in the first full breath she'd inhaled since the men had set upon them.

She peered back at the man cradling his arm. "You nearly killed him." Not far to the left and the man would be dead.

"I missed," Knight muttered.

Louisa met his gaze. No wry amusement crinkled his eyes. His jaw was set, his dark eyes hard as stone. Sometimes she thought there was more to Knight than a ruthless henchman, but times like this proved her wrong.

"You did well," he told her. Knight motioned to the driver. "Let's get moving."

All three men were out of commission. The one who held her captive remained kneeling on the floor, his hand clamped over his arm. With the others senseless, it was clear they were no longer a threat.

"But your back." Even from where she was, she could see blood staining his clothing.

Knight shook his head. "It's a scratch."

She snatched his arm and forced him to twist away so she could view the torn layers. The knife must have been sharp as it had sliced through his jacket and shirt. She peeled apart the fabric and grimaced.

"It is not deep but it needs cleaning."

Knight shook his head again. "That can wait. I have no intention of remaining here any longer. We have no idea if they have any accomplices. These sorts travel in large groups."

"And here I thought all the stories were of lone highwaymen."

"Any lone highwayman is a fool and would be dead the instant he held up a vehicle." Knight snorted. "Not much of a story."

She eyed the cut again and quickly untied the fischu from around her neck. "Stay still," she ordered and pressed the fabric through the slice in his clothes and against the cut. He hissed.

"That will stem the bleeding if you just rest on it." She lifted his hand and pressed it over his lower back to keep it in place.

He did as he was ordered, even if he did look disgruntled doing it. "Now we really must move on."

Nodding, Louisa accepted Knight's help in climbing into the carriage and set her gaze on the interior.

Arms wrapped about herself, she focused on her heavily thudding heart while the carriage moved forward once more. Each long breath she took slowed the beat until she could almost feel all her limbs again and hear everything over the sound of her own pulse. She shook her head to herself.

"I am sorry you had to be involved in that situation."

She realized Knight had been watching her. "I was not shaking my head at that. More at myself." She motioned out of the window. "I deal with men like that all the time—well, similar to that. Men who think they can do what they wish in my inn. But today..."

"Today you were not in your inn," he pointed out.

She sighed. "I suppose you are right. It's different when you are in your own territory. Not that you seemed to have a problem."

"I am used to fighting in enemy territory."

He drew out the pistol case from beneath the seat and loaded the weapon with gunpowder and shot, performing the movements with practiced ease, despite the uneven ground that made the carriage rock.

Louisa swallowed. "You expect more highwaymen?"

He shrugged. "We are in a fine carriage. It is bound to attract attention." His gaze darted briefly over her. "There is no need to be scared. I will keep you safe."

The words were said with scarce emotion or passion but she believed him. He'd already proved he would at the inn and now on the road. She did not much like the idea of having to be protected but she had little choice at present.

"The driver says there's a traveler's inn at Taunton. We should reach there by nightfall and then we'll only be about a day's travel from Bristol."

And then she would be on her own. She clamped her arms back around her waist. The sooner this sorry situation was sorted, the better. Only a day away from home and they had been set upon by highwaymen, and Knight had been injured. She already missed the bustle of her inn and the reassurance of routine. With any luck, she'd prove this man an imposter and be on her way home in no time.

Chapter Seven

"I shall take the floor."

Louisa folded her arms and lifted her chin. Knight groaned inwardly. He'd seen that stance many a time, usually when she was in the process of facing a drunken chap who was begging for another ale. Of course, the drunken chap never won.

But he'd be damned if he'd lose to her. Sharing a room with the woman was enough to addle him as it was. He needed to stay strong. Curse the highwaymen who took up too much time. If they'd arrived earlier, they would not have been forced to share a room. But Louisa was drained by the day—he could see it in her eyes even if she claimed she could travel many more hours—and she needed rest. No doubt their encounter with those black-guards had taken its toll.

"First you are going to take off your shirt so I can look at your wound. Then you are going to lie on the bed and you are going to stay there." She met his gaze head on.

"Like hell." He bit the words out.

Taking several steps toward him, she kept her gaze fixed firmly on his. The journey and their brief clash with those crooks had left her a little rumpled. The curl of fair hair that kept sliding across her forehead made his fingers itch with the need to push it back and steal a fleeting feel of her smooth skin. Her eyes were bright with determination, however, and he could not rely on her fatigue to help him win this battle. He stared into green eyes flecked with hazel and inhaled.

"Let me look," she demanded, taking another pace forward and reaching for his jacket.

He jumped back as her fingers skimmed the garment.

Her lips tilted. "Am I really going to have to chase you around the room?"

It was ridiculous running away from this diminutive woman but it was bad enough they had to share a room. If he removed his shirt, there would be several things that would happen. Firstly, she would see the full extent of his scars up close, and he was not certain he could bear the horrified look on her face when she saw him displayed in his full state of repulsiveness. Secondly, if she touched him, he was doubtful he'd survive it. Even now, if he closed his eyes he could picture her fingers travelling across his skin and it made him ache with need.

"I am well enough," he muttered.

It was true. In a way. The sting from the slice made his skin itch and it needed cleaning but it would not kill him. It took more than a graze to end him or else he'd have died long ago.

"Knight." She reached for him again, moving quickly, and snagged the lapel of his jacket. Louisa used the opportunity to grab the other one and effectively trap him.

When he tried to pull back, she stumbled with him, falling against him. He froze, his breaths laboring in his lungs. The flame in the lantern behind him protested all the movement and flickered and danced, the amber light caressing Louisa's features.

It highlighted her lips, the smooth curve of her cheeks, and the warmth in her eyes. It made him weaker with every second.

He swallowed hard. "You will not leave me in peace on this, will you?"

Her lips curved. "You are learning."

Closing his eyes briefly, he removed her hands from his jacket, all too aware of how perfect her dainty hands felt against his large ones. He shrugged out of his jacket and hesitated. Louisa had seen him shirtless only a day ago, but he hadn't given her time to peruse him, and he had not had time to view her reaction to him. Would he horrify her?

He rotated and undid his cuffs then the button at his neck. Muscles tight, he hauled the shirt over his head and tossed it onto the armoire in front of him. He stared sightlessly out of the window. Her steady breaths and the slight rustle of fabric echoed in his ears as she stepped closer.

Cool fingers touched his back. He inhaled sharply.

"Forgive me."

He couldn't tell her it wasn't the temperature of her fingers that made him shake but the feel of them. As a hard-working woman, they were slightly rough but still about the softest thing to touch his skin in a long time. Her fingers danced a path down his spine and lingered around where the sting of the slice was. He felt her breath following that path and he clenched his palms at his sides.

He closed his eyes again. His muscles quivered with tension. This needed to be over—with haste. How much longer could he survive her sweet touch? It made his gut ache and reminded him of the years spent lusting after her. In all that time, he'd avoided ever being in an intimate situation like this with her. And this was why. It was pure. Damn. Torture.

"It is not too terrible. A little water will do the job."

Jaw clenched, he listened to her pad over to the washbowl and pour some water.

"This will be cold," she warned.

Knight said nothing. He focused on drawing each breath in and out and bracing again for her touch. He shuddered when her fingers framed the cut and hissed at the feel of the cold cloth on his skin. The cool water trickling down his back was at least a welcome distraction from her tender touches.

Mere moments passed but it felt like an eternity. Her fingers left his skin, and he cursed himself inwardly for instantly missing her touch. He reached for his shirt before she could murmur that she was done.

Thrusting it over his head, he twisted back to face her and tugged it down over his abdomen. "Thank you," he said gruffly. He fumbled with the buttons at the cuffs and spotted color in her cheeks.

"Let me," she offered, not giving him a chance to refuse.

Not that he could.

He lifted his arm like a puppet pulled by strings, powerless to do anything but obey.

Biting down on her lip, she pushed the button through the hole then turned her attention to the other cuff, her lashes lowered and fanned across her cheeks.

It gave him far too much unhindered time to study her. At the inn, she never stood still. The bloody woman worked too hard. He didn't think he had ever had the chance to truly look at her.

All it did was confirm everything he'd been thinking.

She was beautiful—the most beautiful woman he'd ever known. Also, she was utterly unaware of her impact on him, which was now a hundred-fold. He tried to drag his gaze away from her and stare at something dull, like the tired-looking wall-paper or the uneven beams. He searched his mind for something tedious of which to think. An absolute void greeted him.

His gaze skipped back to her features, to her plump lips now slightly glossy from where she had bitten down on them, to the barely there freckles on her nose and skimming the sides of her forehead, to that damned curl moving with her every breath, touching her skin as he wished to.

She straightened his cuff and stepped back. "You should rest. I shall have some food sent up."

He blinked. "No." The word escaped him, coarse and gruff.

Louisa lifted a brow. "We both need to eat. It has been a long, tiring day."

Obviously they did. He was used to eating as and when but his body needed plenty of fuel so he did not opt to go hungry unless necessary.

He scowled. "You should not go down there unaccompanied."

Her responding smile was soft. "Knight, I think you forget how I make my living. I have seen and been around far worse." She gave his shoulder a nudge with her palm. "You rest, I shall not be long."

She left the room whilst he was still reeling from that simple, teasing touch. He could have gone after her—after all he was not severely injured—but he could not will his legs to move. She'd meant nothing by any of it and yet he could still sense where her fingers had connected with his skin. Hell fire, he would kill Red when he returned home. If Red's plan had been to drive him to the edge of reason, he was succeeding.

He glanced around the room and at the small bed. He'd crush the blasted thing if he tried to sleep on it. As it was, he had to duck to avoid each beam in the ceiling. Perhaps, if she fell asleep, he could sneak downstairs and sleep in the taproom. He nodded to himself. That sounded like the best way to deal with this situation.

Louisa returned with two bowls of something hot and fragrant. Steam rose from the bowls and made his stomach grumble. She chuckled as the sound cracked the silence of the room. Pushing the door shut behind her with a foot, she handed him a bowl and lowered herself onto the edge of the bed.

Peering around, Knight scowled. There were few places for him to sit in the room, and he doubted the delicate cane-work chair would support his weight or was even large enough for his broad form.

He could eat standing, but he'd look a bloody fool.

Louisa peeked up at him. "Oh. You sit on the bed, I shall sit there."

He opened his mouth to protest but he was not certain why, so he closed it again. It made far more sense for Louisa to sit on the tiny chair. He nodded and carried his bowl over to the bed, sinking onto it and wincing when the mattress creaked. The bed held, however. Perhaps it was stronger than he had originally thought.

She settled herself into the chair and faced him. It was then he comprehended why he had no wish to sit on the bed. As he tore off a chunk of the bread that had been half-dunked into the fragrant stew, it brought to mind all the things he would do with Louisa on a bed if he had the opportunity. Images of soft curves against his hardness, of pale skin touching his sun-kissed body, of heat and need burned through his mind. He shook the images away and focused on the bowl in his palm.

He devoured the bread and finished the stew in a few quick spoonfuls. When he looked up, he found Louisa watching him with amusement while she was still finishing the bread.

"Hungry?"

He lifted a shoulder. "It's a habit."

"From the Army?

He eyed her. "How did you figure that out?"

"You avoided my question about how you knew how the Army operated earlier today, not to mention you eat like a man who will never eat again. Drake eats similarly. Besides, not many civilian men have scars like you."

He stiffened. She'd noticed. Of course she'd damn well noticed. They were hardly tiny scars. One too many close encounters with the French had left him bruised, cut, and beaten. As one of the large men in his unit, he'd often been tasked with leading the run into the fray. His body made an excellent target for rifles too, and he'd even survived being struck by shrapnel from a cannon blast twice. It would have been impossible to escape unscathed.

"Forgive me. I should not have said anything."

Her contrite expression sent a dart of guilt through him. He shook his head. "It is well enough. War is a brutal affair, that is all."

"Have you ever told Julianna about your experiences?"

He shook his head. "It is not for women to know about."

"I know for certain she thinks differently. She is desperate to learn about what you were doing during your time apart."

He grunted. Scrabbling to survive mostly. Once his father disinherited him, he'd travelled south looking for work and stumbled into joining the Army, starting at the very bottom. If he'd possessed any money, he could have bought a commission, but with no coin, he had to take what was offered. At the time, he didn't much care. It gave him something to focus on, and he was hideously good at war.

"Men go to war to protect women. I would not burden Julianna with the knowledge of the reality of it."

Her eyes crinkled, and she set the bowl aside. "I'm not certain why men go to war, but I doubt it is always to protect women."

Knight stood and gathered up her bowl, setting them onto the armoire. "Many of the men I met fought for their women—for the coin it brought to send home or to protect them from a French invasion. Some fought for the thirst for blood. Others had little idea why they were fighting."

"And what were you fighting for?"

He did not answer. She would probably not like his response. He did not fight for honor or to protect those he loved. After his first battle, he was one of those who was thirsty. A tiny taste of it and all he wanted to do was fight more, to unleash every ounce of anger at his father on Frenchmen who had little idea why they were fighting either.

He closed the shutters over the windows. "It is getting late. You should rest."

"You are the one who should be resting."

"It is a mere graze," he insisted.

Hands to her hips, she stared him down. "If this is where you tell me you are too much of a gentleman to share the bed with me, I shall call you a liar. I am a widowed woman and hardly susceptible to ruination."

"And I am no gentleman," he finished for her.

"Well, you are a viscount but..."

"I can sleep on the floor."

She shook her head vigorously. "You need proper rest after today, and I will not have you on the dirty floor with that cut."

"Damn it, woman."

Amusement flickered in her gaze. Why Louisa was never daunted by him, he did not know. Few women would stand up to him like she did. The only exception he could think of was Mrs. Bell from the village who invited him for tea and cake ever since he'd been forced to stop for tea when they were making enquiries a while ago.

But the frail Mrs. Bell did not make impossible demands of him.

"Knight, we are two grown adults and I need a comfortable bed tonight, just as you do. Let us not fight over something so trivial."

The woman had to sound so reasonable, did she not? He blew out a breath and nodded. "Very well."

They readied themselves for bed by kicking off their boots, and Louisa removed her gown, leaving her in a modest, long chemise, but he remained pretty much clothed. Knight eased himself onto the bed and faced the window. Though he could not see her, he heard her bare feet padding across the floorboards while she did whatever it was women did before bed. With a puff, the room was blanketed in darkness. He closed his eyes and the bed dipped beside him.

He waited, body tense while she settled. Once her breaths grew steady and her body softened into his back, he let his muscles loosen.

Knight awakened to a quiet moan and a body curled up against his front. He had to take a moment to orientate himself, scanning the darkened room and noting the faint outlines of the furniture. Then the silhouette of the person in his arms.

He had little idea how, but he had fallen asleep and was now facing Louisa. An arm about her waist, he held her close and she had curled a hand around his biceps. He suspected her eyes were still closed but she wriggled closer and looped a leg around his, drawing him into her warmth. He had to bite back a groan. She could have no idea how long it had been since he'd held a woman and how ridiculously perfect she felt. Every inch of her was soft and warm and giving.

His body responded, and he failed to hold back the growl threatening to burst from his throat. However, the primitive noise was cut off when she lifted her face to his and pressed whisper soft lips to his. Every muscle in his body tight, he dared not breathe, dared not shatter the moment.

Louisa moved her mouth across his and coiled herself closer, until not a single sliver of air existed between them. His body flamed in response. By some miracle, he managed not to respond. She could not realize it was him. She was dreaming of some other man perhaps. Somehow, he would have to wake her and put an end to this madness.

He focused on the arm banding about her waist first. If he just removed that, perhaps he could widen the gap between them and ease out of her hold. But he'd be damned if he could force that arm to move. Each fiber of his being fought him on it, especially when she pressed the kiss harder and emitted a tiny moan. The sound ate deep inside him, and he knew it would haunt him for an eternity.

"Louisa," he rasped out.

She stilled. He made out the fluttering of her eyelashes when she drew back. In the murky light of the room, her gaze met his. Moments passed, punctuated by his frenetic heartbeat in his ears. His arm was still about her, her leg remained wrapped over his. He felt her warm breaths on his skin.

"Knight," she murmured, the word whispering through the air and landing deep in his chest, almost painful in how welcome it was.

He could not be sure who made the first move. Any questions he had faded into obscurity when their lips met again, this time hard and frantic. He pushed a hand into her hair and clasped her to him. She gasped, opening her mouth to his, and he kissed her hungrily, drawing in the sweet taste of her.

Her body undulated into him. Knight could hardly fathom it. Were these really Louisa's hands scrabbling across his body? Tugging at his shirt and trying to find access to his skin? Was this her mouth, sliding its way across his jaw and making his body hurt with need?

He pressed the kiss deep, forcing another moan from her. There was no doubting this was her. And by some miracle, she wanted him. He slid the hand from her hair, down her waist, and bunched up the long chemise she wore. He'd managed not to think about how close he was to skin when they went to bed.

Until now.

Now he realized he was but a slip of fabric from a soft, feminine body—a body he wished he could see better. Too many nights had been passed imagining what she would look like. But he forgot any regret when his fingers met her thigh. He flexed his hand up and around and found the curve of her rear. Her gasps between kisses drove him on, and he cupped her, drawing her closer to him.

"Knight," she breathed.

He trailed kisses down her neck and tugged at the string bunching the neckline of her chemise free to give him better access to her body. She rolled onto her back, her hands to his shoulders, drawing him with her.

"I am too big," he protested in a harsh whisper.

"No."

He could not fight her. The feel of her pliable body hard against his obliterated any sensible thought. Flames licked through him, igniting the years of desire he'd been crushing. There was no going back now.

"Take me," she begged, lifting her hips to his.

This was not how it should be. He should take it slow. Ensure her pleasure. Explore every part of her with care and reverence.

Louisa had other ideas, and he could not fight the tide. He thrust her chemise high and opened the placket of his breeches. She sifted her hands through his hair, pulling him tight against her and urging him on with scattered kisses that left little scalding points in their wake.

He drew back for the briefest moment to meet her gaze. She was but a shadowy outline but he saw enough. She wanted this as much as he. How this had come to be, he could not fathom, nor could he dwell on it any longer.

A hand to her hip, he joined them in a sharp, swift movement that had him clenching his jaw. She inhaled sharply, and her fingernails dug into his arms, the sharp bite of them assuring him this was indeed real. Her heat closed about him, and he had to remind himself to breathe.

"Kiss me."

He relaxed a little, easing down on top of her and seeking out her mouth with his. She opened her lips to him and wrapped her legs about his hips. Louisa drew him deeper, and he clenched his eyes shut. She could have no idea what she was doing to him, how many times he'd imagined such a moment.

His imagination had not done her justice. He could never have predicted her fiery response—though he should have done. She rocked her hips up into his. He responded with a thrust, and she cried out. The noise impelled him on. He drove deep into her, relishing every tremor and stuttered breath. Her responding kisses were wild and erratic.

Knight increased the pace, a hand under her rear, and was utterly lost to her. Kissing her hard, he buried his head into the crook of her neck and drank in the sweet, clean fragrance of her while he kept up the frantic rhythm with little finesse.

It did not seem to matter. Her nails raked down his arms and her breaths grew heavy. She tensed underneath him, her cries increased. He gritted his teeth and dragged her over the edge until her body tightened and released, making him feel a mere second away from exploding. He held on, drawing out her peak until she relaxed then withdrew quickly, and with a harsh, hot breath, his eyes clenched tightly shut, he spilled into his hand and onto her bare thigh. A wave of relief flowed over him, and he opened his eyes.

In the darkness, he could make out the satisfied shape of her, her hands sprawled on either side of her head, her fingers loose and relaxed. The inevitable prod of regret needled at him. Louisa deserved better than a scarred, sullen bastard like him.

"I—"

A long inhale from Louisa and the sound of her rolling over cut him off. Not that he knew what he could possibly say. *Forgive me,* perhaps. Or some excuse for his moment of weakness. And apologize for not being softer, for not taking his time. But she saved him from any response with a heavy exhale. He allowed himself a small smile at her sleeping form.

He cleaned himself up and gingerly dabbed her thigh with a cloth, erasing any evidence of their moment together. After tucking her under the blankets, he allowed himself one last moment of weakness and swept a gentle kiss across her forehead.

Knight straightened his clothing and shook his head to himself. This had been one big, big mistake. He'd have to do better tomorrow. For her sake and for his.

Chapter Eight

With shaky hands, Louisa buttoned up her gown. The trouble was, she could not quite figure out if the shaking was from anger or something else. From the memory of what had happened perhaps. She skimmed a finger over a red mark above one breast—evidence of Knight's rough stubble. If it were not for the ache between her thighs and that mark, she could have been led to believe it had all been a dream.

She shook her head. No. She could never have dreamed such a thing. As much as Knight plagued her thoughts, she'd been hard-pressed to imagine what it would be like to make love to such a man. Would he be tender? Skilled? Rough?

He'd been none of those things. They'd both been utterly swept away, and it had been hard, fast, and furious. And her body had responded like it never had before. There had been no skill from either of them, no game of seduction. The only thing that had driven them both over the edge was a fiery passion she had not known Knight possessed.

Swallowing, she did up the last button and eyed the empty bed. A passion he wanted to forget clearly, if his disappearance from the room had anything to do with it. No doubt he was down in the taproom, indulging in an ale or something stronger.

A hand to the back of her neck, she blew out a breath and pressed fingers into the ache gathering at the top of her spine. This whole thing was giving her a headache. She wanted to go back a few days when everything was simple. The inn was still hers, Ralph had not appeared in Cornwall, and she had no idea what it would be like to make love to Knight. Of all the people to take as a lover, why did it have to be him?

Because you have never been interested in anyone else, whispered a voice.

She scowled at the voice. It was true. She had been too busy ensuring the inn became, and remained, profitable. There had been a few interested men and, as a widow, she could have taken a lover without impunity. However, one needed time to take a lover. Something she never had.

Louisa snatched up a hairbrush from her bag and tugged it viciously through her hair as though the pain tingling her scalp might help her forget what had happened. It had all been her fault too. He'd given her every opportunity to deny him, to kick him from the bed, and yet she could not resist. Lord, what had happened to her simple life of merely wondering about the brooding man?

Of course, now she did not have to wonder any longer. Now she knew what his lips felt like on hers, how he tasted, how wonderful his rough palms were against her skin. As she looped her hair up and jabbed pins in it, she walked over to the window and eyed her fuzzy reflection in it. Without a mirror in the room, it would have to do. She looked presentable enough to travel, she reckoned.

They did not have far to go to Bristol now. Another day's travel at best. Once they were there, she could send Knight on his way to Northumberland and catch a mail coach back to Penshallow once she'd found out whatever she could about Ralph.

She only hoped her instincts were correct and this man was not her stepson after all. If he was truly Ralph, she had little idea what she would do without her living. She had some money but hardly enough to set up a new business. And it was not as though she had other skills. Running an inn was all she had ever known.

Straightening her shoulders, she exhaled slowly. There was no more putting it off. She would have to face Knight at some point. Ensuring her belongings were packed neatly, she grabbed her bag and studied the room. Were it not for the rumpled bed, there would be no evidence of Knight at all. He must have gathered up his belongings too so he would not even have to step foot back in the room. It should not hurt but it needled at her heart that he wanted to escape her.

Even if it should not. She needed to forget about last night too. After all, she had much bigger things to worry about.

Making her way downstairs, she stepped into the already busy taproom. Though few guests were awake, the familiar sight of an inn readying itself for the day with delivery boys hauling in boxes and drivers eating their morning meals before their employees could arise, made her heart ache further for home.

She spotted Knight, his elbows propped on the bar, a clean shirt stretched over broad shoulders. A half-empty ale sat in front of him. He spotted her and something flickered in his gaze—a flash of desire maybe—but he shuttered it quickly, adopting his usual gruff expression. She lifted her chin. That was fine with her. She needed to forget what happened just as much as he.

"Good morning," she said, forcing a bright note into her voice.

Confusion briefly creased his brow before vanishing. Perhaps he'd expected her to be angry. She was really. An irrational part of her had wanted to wake in his arms and enjoy his kisses and body in the daylight. Really, she should be grateful he had run away. He had saved her from making a fool of herself and dragging this on longer than it should.

He glanced at her bag. "You're ready to leave?"

She nodded. The sooner they left this place, the better. Then they could go their separate ways and forget this ever happened.

"Do you not want to eat?" he asked.

"No."

She answered before really considering her body's state, but she doubted she could bring herself to eat anything in front of him. Even now, she was recalling how his hands had felt on her body, how the heavy weight of him on top of her had been so perfectly right. She even vaguely recalled how he'd tucked her exhausted body into bed and brushed a kiss across her forehead. Unfortunately—or perhaps fortunately—she'd been so sated, she could not even respond to his tender touches.

He shrugged. "Very well, let us get moving. The carriage is ready."

He took her travel bag from her before she could protest and headed outside. She hurried to catch up and found the carriage along with the driver and footmen waiting in the courtyard. Whether they were simply being efficient or Knight had ordered them to make ready swiftly, she did not know, but she suspected the latter.

"I know you need to get to Bristol with haste," he muttered.

Louisa nodded, not willing to call him out on his excuse. It was true, though. The sooner she found out what she could about Ralph, the better.

Knight offered a hand to aid her into the carriage and she hesitated in taking it. He quickly withdrew it and glanced away. Blowing out a breath, she stepped into the vehicle and slid onto the seat. They would be on the road for most of the day, which would feel like a long journey normally, but it was going to feel even worse if they did not discuss what had happened, no matter how uncomfortable it felt to address what happened between them.

He entered the carriage and settled opposite her. Rapping his knuckles on the roof, he folded his arms across his wide chest and turned his attention to the view outside. Louisa did the same while they travelled through the carriage entrance and turned into the road. Few other carriages were on the road but several carts were moving to and from the inn, slowing their progress out into the surrounding countryside.

Despite the fresh air drifting in through the open window and the hints of sunshine shining through the diaphanous clouds, the air in the carriage seemed thick and unyielding. Louisa eyed Knight. He still avoided her gaze and it gave her an opportunity to study him. Whatever had happened during the war left him more scarred than most men. She'd seen the scars before from a distance but never been able to touch them or view them closely. Thanks to running an inn, she recognized some of the marks as wounds created by blades and others as gunshot wounds. The thought of him suffering so much pain made her want to fling herself at him and soothe away any memory of it.

He met her gaze, breaking such ridiculous thoughts. Though he swung his attention quickly from her, she cleared her throat, forcing him to look at her again.

"Knight," she started, clenching her fists and willing her silly heart to slow. She tried again. "Knight, about what happened..."

"Louisa," he said, warning clear in his tone.

"You have nothing to fear," she blurted. "I want nothing from you."

No doubt he thought her some irrational woman who would expect romance and marriage. She knew Knight was not the sort of man to want to settle down just as she was far too busy to think on such things.

His brow furrowed.

"It was one moment, that is all." Her cheeks felt hot with the lie.

"It will not happen again."

She forced a smile. "Exactly. We shall just forget it ever happened and not mention it again."

He gave a stiff nod, opened his mouth to say something, then shut it again. If she was waiting for something more from him, he would not give her anything more. Which was fine with her. The less they talked, the better. Once they were back in Cornwall, they hardly needed to interact anyway. That was, so long as she still owned an inn by then.

And he had not taken up the role of viscount in Northumberland. For all she knew, he might decide he should remain there and somehow save the estate.

"What do you intend to do when you arrive?" he asked as they passed the twenty-mile marker to Bristol—the first full sentence he'd uttered in ages.

Louisa pressed her lips together. When she'd decided to take Red up on his offer, she had not really thought it through. She did not know Bristol at all and had little idea where she should start.

"I thought I might ask around at whichever inn I stay in and see if anyone knows of him."

Knight scowled. "Bristol is a big place. It shall not be that easy."

"There is always the sawmill. Ralph said he worked there. Maybe someone there will know something."

His expression darkened. "Bristol is a large town, not like Penshallow."

Louisa hardly knew how to respond and did not quite understand the statement until they began to travel through the town toward the center, where one of the drivers knew of a reputable but not too expensive traveler's inn. Houses were clustered close together and the roads thick with carts and carriages. Signs of industry were everywhere and shops cluttered up the central streets. A blanket of smoke hung over the town, turned an ominous murky amber color from the setting sun.

The carriage drew into a cobbled courtyard and Louisa peered up at the sizeable inn. The stables appeared almost full and men hastened back and forth, bringing food and water to the horses. She grimaced. Her time looking after a pub should have prepared her for anything, but in Bristol, she felt wide-eyed and innocent. This place was nothing like her simple inn.

"Well..." she started.

The driver opened the door, leaving Louisa little opportunity to say anything to Knight. Not that she knew what to say. *Thank you for the sullen company? Sorry we can no longer be friends because we shared a passionate night together? Good luck with the whole viscount affair?*

What did one even say to a lover?

He stepped out behind her and took her bag from the driver before she could reach for it. He motioned for his bag too, and Louisa eyed him. "What—"

"I am staying with you."

"But—"

"Bristol is no place for a woman on her own, and I am in no hurry."

His tone brokered no argument, and as much as she would have liked to remind him she was no weakling in need of a man's protection, Louisa did not have it in her—nor was she foolish enough to deny his aid.

"I shall ensure there are enough rooms," he muttered, leading the way into the inn.

Louisa did not know whether to laugh or cry. A slightly hysterical laugh escaped her, which she supposed was better than weeping, and Knight gave her an odd look.

"Yes, excellent idea." She cringed at her overly bright tone. Did he know? Could he tell that she secretly hoped there would not be enough rooms again?

What a fool she was.

Chapter Nine

Knight eyed the bed with distaste. He'd hardly slept a wink thanks to its narrow frame. His bloody feet kept getting tangled in the metal bars at the end and he'd nearly rolled off several times. He yawned and dragged himself over to the wash-bowl to give himself a thorough wash in the freezing water. If that did not wake him, nothing would.

Unfortunately, he could not only blame the bed for his lack of sleep.

He dipped the washcloth in the water and rubbed it across his chest and arms, shuddering as icy trickles tracked down his back. Maybe the cold would knock some sense into him. It was not the first time he had slept on a tiny bed, but it was the first time he'd done so after sharing a bed with Louisa. Foolishly, he missed her body nestled up to him. And, naturally, he could not remove the memory of what had happened between them. Little flickers of it kept haunting him—the feel of her lips, the curve of her body, the sensuous noises she made.

He exhaled heavily and washed his face vigorously, rubbing his hands over the increasing stubble on his jaw. It would have been easier to take the carriage and move on—get this blasted estate business done and return to Cornwall to meet Drake as he returned and plan their next move.

After drying his face and body, he picked up his clothes and dressed quickly. He dared not leave Louisa alone for long in a place like this. He'd seen her wide eyes and known he could not go. While the inn might be reputable, there was plenty of danger to be found in a large town like this. People would take one look at her and know they could take advantage. As strong as she was on her own territory, it was entirely different here.

Running fingers through his hair, he donned his jacket, shoved his feet into boots, and followed the narrow corridor to Louisa's room—just a few doors down. He might have liked to have her next to him for safety's sake but the division between them at least meant he could not hear her shuffling around through the thin walls.

He snorted to himself. What a fine job he was doing, of forgetting the whole sorry mess. She'd made it clear it was a mistake. Perhaps she needed comforting. Or something else. Whatever the reason, it would not happen again.

Louisa opened her door before he could knock. She stumbled back slightly at the sight of him. "Oh." She smiled. "You startled me."

"I came to see if you were ready."

"Yes." She adjusted her straw bonnet, and Knight could not help but stare at the whole effect.

He was so damned used to her in nothing but a simple gown and an apron. Not even her travelling clothes were quite like this. No, it might not be as fine as something worn by Red's wife or his sister-in-law, but the careful cut of the gown emphasized her curves, and the tiny dotted pattern on it forced his gaze up and down the length of her. Underneath the bonnet, curls sprung out around her neck. His heart quickened its beat.

"I know I look ridiculous." She gave a rueful smile, and her cheeks reddened.

"You look beautiful." The statement escaped him swiftly before he could force it back.

Her gaze shot to his. "Oh."

"That is..."

"Um, thank you."

He nodded stiffly, uncertain how to respond. He did not make a habit of complimenting women.

"I have asked around and there's only one sawmill. It is on..." She frowned and pressed fingers to her forehead. "Oh, blast, I cannot recall which road the gentleman said."

"Colebrook Road?"

"Yes!" She paused. "How did you know?"

"I asked around last night."

Hands to her hips, she eyed him. "I suppose this is the part where you tell me I am not to go alone. And that is why you have not buttoned your shirt or bothered with a cravat?"

Knight peered down. The cravat, he was not been worried about. If they were to step foot in some of the rougher parts of town, the last thing he needed was to look like a dandy. However, he had not realized he'd neglected to even button his shirt. He went to do it up, but Louisa stepped closer and reached up to button it for him.

He snatched her hand midair, and she froze. Her fingers were soft in his, cradled perfectly in his hand. He remembered them on his body, the rough pads of her fingertips contrasting with the softness of her palms as they slid over his back. Her gaze locked onto his and her lips parted. As he stared into those mossy green eyes, her pupils widened. Surely she could not desire him? Surely their night together had been a moment of madness on her behalf? Perhaps it was on his too but borne of a desire for her that had been building for years. There was no chance she felt the same.

Did she?

Her throat worked, and he released her hand, swiftly doing up the button at his neck. The only reason he neglected it had been because he was thinking of her as he'd dressed. She certainly did not need to know that.

"I will be accompanying you, yes," he said, his voice hoarse.

"You are lucky I do not have the energy to fight you today." Her lips curved, but he saw uncertainty flicker in her eyes as she rubbed where he'd touched her with the other hand. "I have already asked for the carriage to be made ready, but the driver will drop us off a few roads away."

He nodded. The last thing they needed was to drive up in a carriage with the crest of the earl on it. No one would give them any information if they thought them gentry.

They left the inn and took the carriage through busy streets. The scent of smoke hung in the air and the road was dense with vehicles. Knight imagined it would take less time on foot but it would also mean running into more unsavory characters, especially as Knight could not claim to know his way around Bristol. The driver had been wise enough to ask for directions at the inn and only stopped once more to confirm them.

"I suppose you might have a carriage of your own after returning to Northumberland."

He peered at her and shook his head. "Anything not entailed to the estate will not be mine. Even if there were one, my father's debts will be great so it shall likely have to be sold off."

"Julianna talked a little of home. She said your father was always spending money he did not have and the house was one of luxury."

"My father was an arrogant fool. He threw away hundreds of years of toil for the latest fashion. If he was not having the house redecorated, he was lavishing money on clothes or his latest mistress."

"Oh." Louisa grimaced. "Julianna never mentioned mistresses."

"She did not know. My father, despite his flaws, was excellent at keeping secrets." He grunted. "The last time I talked to him, he had purchased a house for his latest mistress."

"That is why you left?"

He shrugged. "Our relationship was never a pleasant one."

There was no need to mention the rest of his father's behavior. Though Louisa would probably understand how Knight had become so good with his fists if he told her. The day Knight left had been the day he'd finally stood up to his father.

The carriage came to a juddering halt, jolting him from his thoughts. He had already told her too much. His whole relationship with his father and the sorry mess he'd left both Knight and Julianna in was better forgotten. Julianna had moved on and was blissfully happy with Drake and her new life in Cornwall. Hopefully when this was done, he could do the same.

There might not be any blissful happiness in his future but he'd settle for returning to Cornwall without the worry his father might one day find him.

They walked the few streets to the mill. The noise of the saws ground through the air and a perpetual cloud of dust surrounded the buildings.

Knight led the way into the courtyard through double gates that towered above them. Louisa craned her neck to peer up at the sign that spanned the doorway, and he saw her mouth *Barburgh Mill*. Sawdust crunched underfoot and logs were stacked taller than Knight up one side of the courtyard. Knight felt the gaze of the workers on them—especially Louisa. Why did the blasted woman have to look so pretty, today of all days?

He spotted what he suspected was the foreman, a pocket watch in hand and his clothing neat and tidy as he watched over the stacking of logs. The man spotted them and hastened over.

"This is no place for a lady. Be gone with you." The man frowned from underneath his cap. Short and slightly wide, he had a thick gray speckled moustache and a generous mouth with teeth stained yellow. From the smell of him, the man indulged in chewing tobacco.

"I just need some information," Louisa started, but the man shook his head.

"Too dangerous here, and I don't have time for conversations with young ladies. You need to leave."

Aware of the gazes still glued to them, Knight kept his senses alert. He stared coldly at the foreman. "The lady only needs to ask a question or two. Give us a few minutes and we shall be on our way."

Running his gaze up and down Knight and finally seeming to take stock of him, the man grunted. "Fine, but I don't have much time, mind." He shoved his pocket watch back into his waistcoat and motioned for them to follow him.

Louisa hurried along beside Knight while he only needed to lengthen his strides to keep up with the surprisingly fast man. He led them into a cramped, dark office occupied by a generous dark wood desk that was smothered in piles of paper. Two windows looked out onto the courtyard, but they were grimy and let in meagre light.

The man folded his arms. "Ask your question then."

Louisa twined her hands together. "I need to know if a man worked here. My, um, stepson—Ralph Carter."

The foreman shook his head. "Never heard of him. Now if that is all..." The man went to leave, but Knight put an arm out in front of him.

"Are you certain?" Knight pressed.

The foreman cocked his head. His moustache bristled. "Yes, I'm certain. I've worked here nearly ten years, and I know every man who works under me."

"He would have worked here quite recently," Louisa explained.

"Ma'am, if your stepson worked one of the mills here, it was not this one. Maybe try Dickson's."

Louisa met Knight's gaze and sighed. "This is the only lumber mill. Maybe I misheard."

"Or you are right and he is not Ralph Carter," Knight suggested.

She pursed her lips. "But this is not definitive proof."

It wasn't. They still had no idea who this man was if he was not Ralph Carter. "Have you had many men leave recently?"

The foreman tugged out his watch, snapped it open, and glared at Knight. When Knight folded his arms and stared him down, the man's shoulders dropped.

"Very few. Barburgh pays almost the highest wage to workers in Bristol." The man lifted his chin and a slight proud smile crept across his lips.

Louisa lifted her head. "Oh, so you would remember any who left recently?"

The man nodded. "I would think so."

"Were any of them tall, clean-shaven? With reddish brown hair?" Louisa asked. "They might have been planning to travel to Cornwall."

The man lifted a brow. "I wouldn't know about clean-shaven but that sounds like Hugh Stanton."

Louisa's eyes lit up. "Can you tell me about him?"

"He said he had come into some money." The man shrugged. "I didn't ask for details. However, his wife is still in Bristol and has been knocking on my gate several times a week asking if Stanton has returned." The man huffed. "A sorry business is that. He won't be coming back and she's six little mouths to feed." He wagged a finger at Louisa. "If you see him, you can tell him he won't be getting his job back. I can find plenty of other eager men to work who don't abandon their wives and children."

Louisa nodded. "Do you happen to know where she lives?"

"Aye, down Broad Street. Another place not suitable for ladies." He glanced at Knight. "Even if you have a protector. This is a big town, ma'am, and it's easy for strangers to go missing."

If Louisa was scared at all, she did not show it. "Thank you for your help, Mr., um…"

The foreman ignored her. "I need to be getting back to work. I trust you'll see yourselves out."

Knight stepped aside and let the man past. "He's fast for a little man," he muttered.

"He was not happy about having us here." Louisa gripped Knight's arm and grinned. "But at least we have information. This Hugh has to be the man impersonating Ralph, do you not think? Which means he is not my stepson and has no claim on the inn!"

"Let us go find his wife before we jump to any conclusions." He paused as he considered the foreman's warning. "Or perhaps you should return to the inn while I go in search of her."

She shook her head vigorously. "Not a chance."

He wasn't surprised, but he had been vaguely hopeful he could deposit Louisa somewhere safe while he continued the investigation. He would not have minded a little time away from her either. She meant nothing by it, but even the small touch to his arm made his skin itch with need.

"Come on then." Knight wasn't going to argue with her. The sooner they found out the truth about this Stanton chap, the better, then they could go their separate ways.

He led the way out of the mill, staring down anyone who dared look at Louisa. Jaw clenched, he put a hand to the small of her back. She jolted slightly and the feel of her stays made him want to curl his fingers around them and rip them asunder to access the sweet flesh below. But these men needed to know Louisa was not theirs to look at.

Unfortunately for him, she was not his either.

Chapter Ten

Though the foreman's warning had infiltrated, Louisa had paid little attention to it. Now she understood what he meant about people going missing. The narrow alleys between buildings in this part of Bristol were gray and grim, and even if nothing untoward happened to a person, it would be easy to get lost and never emerge again.

A film of dirt clung to everything—the walls, the windows, even the ragged clothing hanging from lines strung between the buildings. Children huddled together in doorways, garments hangings from boney bodies while weary parents with a sheen of hopelessness in their eyes stood behind them, their gazes tracking Louisa and Knight's movements.

She was no stranger to poverty—it existed in the bigger towns in Cornwall—and she had hardly grown up wealthy. Many a day, she'd been forced to go hungry. But her life had been full of fresh air and the opportunity to escape into the countryside and forget the hunger pangs for a while.

Knight took her arm and looped it through his. As much as his proximity made her breathless, she was grateful for his protection. Crime had to be rife in this area.

"This is it—Broad Street." He nodded at the worn sign nailed to one of the gray stone buildings.

"We shall have to ask someone if they know Mrs. Stanton."

Knight nodded toward a woman sitting on a doorstep, weaving reeds into a basket shape. "I shall—"

Louisa tugged on his arm to hold him back. "I shall go and ask. You will probably frighten the life out of her."

He gave a resigned nod and released her arm. Louisa fished in her pocket for one of the few coins she had on her person and folded it into her palm. "Excuse me?"

The woman ignored her, dirty face wrinkled in concentration. Louisa revealed the coin and the woman peered up and narrowed her gaze.

"Do you know where Mrs. Stanton lives?"

"Aye, just down there. The house on the corner." The woman waved a hand farther down the alley then thrust the hand out, palm open.

Louisa placed the coin in her palm, which vanished into the woman's clutch before Louisa could say thank you. The woman turned her attention back to the basket so Louisa returned to Knight and led him toward the house the woman had motioned to.

The dwelling barely counted as a house in Louisa's estimation. Split into two by a set of stairs on the outside leading to another front door, it was narrow, with one window for each story. Louisa knocked on the door, whispering to Knight to stand back. If anyone saw him in their doorway, they would never answer.

Several faces pressed against the grimy glass and the door squeaked open an inch or so, allowing Louisa to just about view the woman behind it.

"Mrs. Stanton? My name is Louisa Carter. I'm hoping you can help me—"

Mrs. Stanton went to push the door shut, but Knight rushed forward and shoved his boot in the gap. "We know where your husband is, Mrs. Stanton."

The woman eased open the door and eyed them both. Thin and young—younger than Louisa—Mrs. Stanton's clothes hung off her body. A child clung to one leg and Louisa heard a baby crying in the background. With stringy red hair hanging in a loose braid around her face, dark circles ringed her eyes and premature flecks of white were already showing in her hair.

"You have spoken to Hugh?" she asked, her voice tremulous.

"Can we come in?" Louisa asked.

Mrs. Stanton ran her gaze up and down Knight.

"He is harmless, I promise," Louisa said with a smile.

"As you will." Mrs. Stanton stepped back, allowing them access to the cramped room.

A bed occupied one side of the room and a table with two chairs took up most of the space. Only one candle was lit on a wall sconce, so it took Louisa's eyes a moment to adjust to the darkness before she spotted the rest of the children. Two sat on the bed while another two boys were fighting in one corner.

"Mrs. Stanton—"

The din of the baby crying and the children fighting prevented her from saying anything further.

"Fight outside," she ordered the two boys and scooped up a squalling baby from a crib on the floor, rocking it until it quietened. The two boys scampered out and the noise in the room decreased enough for Louisa to be heard.

"I met your husband in Cornwall. At least I think he is your husband. He was going by another name," Louisa explained. "Mrs. Stanton, can you tell me if your husband said anything to you before he left?"

"Call me Abigail," she said as she sank onto one of the chairs. "Mrs. Stanton makes me sound old."

Louisa sat opposite her while Knight attempted to slink into the shadows by the door, but one of the boys on the bed jumped down and walked over to him, holding up his arms. "Up!" the little boy demanded.

Abigail gave a weak smile. "George likes to be high up and you are very tall."

Knight looked between Louisa, Abigail, and the boy then gave a huff. Reaching down, he picked up the boy with ease and held him at chest height. George wrapped his arms around Knight's neck, and Louisa had to prevent a smile appearing on her lips at Knight's startled expression.

"I don't know what Hugh is up to," Abigail admitted. "He's...he's been distant lately. Drinking a lot, spending money on whores." She shrugged. "He always made sure we had food on the table, though. Always." She jabbed a finger against the table.

"Did he tell you where he was going?" Louisa asked.

Abigail rubbed her brow. "He muttered something about coming across a fortune. I didn't think he'd leave us, though." She looked up at the little boy in Knight's arms. "I don't know how much longer we can survive without income."

Louisa met Knight's grim gaze. If Ralph—or perhaps she should call him Hugh as she was growing certain that was who he was—wanted to take over the inn, there was no chance he was coming back, and from the sounds of his behavior, he had little intention of aiding Abigail at all.

"Would he have told anyone else about his plans?" Knight pressed.

"Maybe Eli Jones. They're always together." Abigail pursed her lips. "He's a bad influence on my Hugh."

Louisa nodded sympathetically. "Where can we find him?"

"The Boar's Head usually. It's not far from here." Abigail jabbed a thumb to her left and glanced over Louisa. "I wouldn't step foot in there if I were you."

Louisa didn't answer. If that was where she could find out more information, then that was where she had to go. Knight lowered the boy down, giving his hair a ruffle. His large hand on the boy's head made Louisa smile. The man had a soft spot for children it seemed.

"We should get going," commented Knight, apparently spotting Louisa's desire to find this Eli.

Louisa nodded and rose. "Thank you for your time, Abigail."

"Will you help me get him back?" pleaded Abigail.

Unsure how to respond, Louisa glanced at Knight. The woman was better off without him, but she and the children would also starve. What sort of a man abandoned his wife and young children with no word and no way to survive?

A man who would try to take an inn that did not belong to him, she supposed.

Drawing out a handful of coins from his inner pocket, Knight dropped them onto the table in front of Abigail. "Look for a new husband," he said. "Yours will not be back."

Louisa waited until they were outside before drawing him to one side. "Did you have to be so...so forthright?"

Knight lifted a shoulder. "He won't return. And if he does, the bastard does not deserve a second chance."

"She seems to care for him."

He met her gaze. "People often care for those they should not."

She looked away, her stomach twisting. Was that a warning? She could not tell, but the words repeated through her mind as they made their way to The Boar's Head, which was indeed as close as Abigail had suggested. Was she starting to care for Knight?

She stole a peek at him. His casual attire and stubbled jaw line were not an uncommon sight in her inn. Being a smuggler hardly called for one to be perfectly groomed. Yet that mild inkling of curiosity about him had increased. Now she not only wondered what it would be like to run a hand across that jaw but also how it would feel against her thighs or her breasts. Their night together had been so hard and fast she'd hardly been able to process it.

And now she wanted more.

She forced her attention to the pub in front of them. Wide with four windows tucked into the eaves of the tiled roof, the outside had once been whitewashed but the color was flecking away to reveal the chunky stone beneath and what white remained was clouded by dirt. The windows were rimmed with chipped black frames. Outside, a man lolled against one of the walls, a cup clasped tight in one hand as though terrified of being parted from it in his drunken state.

"I should have thrown you over my shoulder and taken you back to the carriage," Knight grumbled.

Lifting a brow, she stared up at him. "You can still try."

He huffed. "Not if I want to keep my—" He hesitated.

"Your?"

"Balls," he muttered.

Louisa laughed. "There's still time, Lewis Knight. There's still time."

Chapter Eleven

Knight ducked a low beam and glared at the next person to eye Louisa. He should have followed through with his threat and slung her over his shoulder to take her back to the carriage. His boots clung to the sticky floor, and he grimaced. He'd set foot in too many inns like this in his time and even Louisa, as hardy as she was, did not belong here.

Damn it, she should be back in Cornwall, running her inn with all her usual confidence. If he got his hands on this bloody Hugh, he'd make sure the bastard never thought of trying to swindle anyone ever again.

"Stay close," he murmured to Louisa.

She nodded and inched toward him, posture stiff. Raucous laughter and conversation ebbed and flowed as Louisa walked past, silencing briefly enough for the men to eye her before they returned to their conversations. She kept her gaze fixed ahead, ignoring all the stares, but she must have felt them. Most looked away as soon as he caught their eye but a few were too drunken to see the threat in his glare. He'd have to watch them lest the alcohol make them bold.

Knight led the way past haphazard furniture to the bar, some broken from what had to be the previous night's fight. Broken glass swept to the sides and a fist-sized hole in the wooden paneling that lined the walls confirmed his theory. A heavy-set man with thick brows and a reddened nose peered up at him, his apron streaked with grease stains.

"What can I be getting you?" He ignored Louisa's presence, and Knight saw Louisa's scowl from the corner of his vision.

Knight pressed a coin across the bar. It might not be needed, but he wanted Louisa out of this wretched place with haste. "I'm looking for Eli Jones."

The man glanced at the coin and palmed it quickly. He nodded toward the rear of the room. Several men were taking part in a game of cards around a small table. Empty glasses scattered about them told him they'd been playing for some time.

Louisa strode over before Knight could stop her. He caught up quickly, but she was already thrusting a finger at one of the men, asking if he was Eli. He smirked and threw back the remnants of an ale, swiping a hand across his face. Droplets of beer still clung to a wiry, ginger beard. His hair was a paler shade of red and his eyes were sunken and bloodshot.

"For you." He winked. "I'll be anything."

Knight hovered over Louisa's shoulder and the soberer of his companions cast their gazes to the table.

"Are you Mr. Jones?" she tried again.

"Does this mean..." He rose from the table, shoving his chair back and sending it toppling over. The leg of the chair caught him and he stumbled before tripping over it. He peeled himself up from the floor and laughed, ignorant to the fact his friends didn't join in. "Does this mean you have heard of my way with the ladies? Because..." His words were so slurred it was hard to make out the rest of his sentence but Knight was certain it was something no woman should hear. He curled a fist.

Louisa gave a frustrated huff. "The man is roaring drunk."

Knight nodded. "You'll get little sense out of him."

Louisa folded her arms. "You are Eli then?"

The movement caused Eli's gaze to focus on her chest. His lips curved. Knight released a hot breath and tightened his jaw. He kept his muscles tense as Eli staggered toward Louisa.

"As I said, I'll be anything you want me to be." Eli hiccupped and swayed into Louisa, grabbing her wrists and drawing her against him while she struggled against his hold. He attempted to drag her around the room in some imitation of a country dance. When he whirled Louisa away, Knight stepped in. He grabbed the man by his collar and hauled him away from Louisa.

Eli released her instantly. "What the—"

Knight dragged the man through the inn. Though patrons tracked his movements, none offered aid. Eli thrashed but it was no more annoying than that of a fly batting against glass. If Knight really wanted to harm the man, it would be easy. One swat and he'd be knocked senseless.

"Knight..." Louisa followed after him as Eli's head knocked against a table leg. "Careful!"

He ignored her. If she didn't like his methods, tough. He was not going to stand around and watch her be pawed by the bastard. Shoving the door open with a foot, he hauled Eli outside and flung him down in the dirt. He glanced around and snatched a bucket out of the water trough in front of the building. Scooping a bucketful of murky water, he tossed it over the man who was struggling to find his feet.

Louisa gasped. Eli fell back to the ground, the dank water pooling on the hard ground around him. He swept a hand over his face and squinted up at Knight. His eyes widened as he scanned Knight's length, and Knight held back a smirk. The frigid water had sobered the man up enough to finally realize what he was up against.

"What the bloody hell do you want with me?" Eli spluttered.

Louisa stepped forward. "We just want to ask a few questions."

Eli attempted to stand again, but his legs gave way and he landed with a splash on the ground. He lifted his arms and let them fall back down to his sides with a sigh. "Ask away."

"Do you know Hugh Stanton?" Louisa asked.

He narrowed his gaze and peered up at them both. "Why do you need to know?"

Knight took a step forward, hands fisted.

Eli's eyes widened, and he held up both palms. "Yes, yes, I know him!"

Louisa folded her arms. "Did you know that he was planning to go to Cornwall?"

"To take something that did not belong to him," Knight muttered under his breath.

Eli glanced around and finally nodded.

"And you know why?" Louisa continued.

"Yes, yes. Something about an inn." He waved a hand. "But what does that have to do with you?"

"That inn is mine." She thrust a thumb toward herself.

"Ah." Eli's third attempt to rise was met with success, and he eased himself up against the water trough, coming to sit on the edge. He raised an arm and grimaced as water dripped from the sleeve. "I imagine that don't make you too happy."

Louisa cocked her head. "He had the deeds to the inn. Do you know how?"

"Look, I had nothing to do with this, understand? We just drink together. Don't mean much." Eli nodded toward Knight. "Make sure he don't kill me, if you'd be so kind, ma'am."

She swung an amused glance at Knight. "If you answer my questions, I will ensure your safety."

"He said he got the papers from an old war friend—Ralph something." Eli screwed up his face. "I don't know much more. Just said he was going to Cornwall to claim the inn as his."

Louisa glanced at Knight. "That's all you know? Are you certain?"

Eli pushed his wet hair from his face. "Yes, I swear on my ma's grave. I know nothing more."

Knight eyed the man, whose gaze shot quickly to the floor. There was hesitation in his expression, and Knight did not like it one jot. He went to reach for him again, but Louisa put a hand to his chest.

"Let him be. We know all we need to know," she murmured. "Though I am not certain how we prove Hugh is not Ralph. If he has the deeds to the inn, he might have other documents of Ralph's. He had a letter from Jack but who knows what else he has."

"Which he could use to prove he is Ralph."

"Which he certainly is not." Louisa shoved a curl from her face. "So now what?"

"His wife," Knight said, tone grim. The woman and her children needed to move on and forget the man who had abandoned them, but Abigail would be able to declare he was her husband in a court of law and ensure that Hugh could place no claim.

Pinching the bridge of her nose, Louisa nodded. "Perhaps I can persuade her to accompany me home somehow."

Knight glanced at the gray skies, thick with the threat of rain, and considered his empty stomach. "We will see what we can do after some rest."

"You intend to stay another day?"

He tensed. That hopeful tone made the hairs on the back of his neck stand on end. Did she really want him to keep her company for longer? He looked away. No, it was simply because he was useful.

"Too late to travel now." He started in the direction of the waiting carriage, forcing her to scurry to catch up and ensuring he did not have to make any further conversation.

By the time they reached the inn, fat droplets of rain beat at the carriage roof, a cacophony of noise that worsened his headache— a headache that had been created by him spending the entire damned day grinding his teeth. If he was not ready to pluck out the eyes of every man who looked at Louisa, he was trying not to think about how he wanted to pull her into his arms and take away the strain of the day. Though they had figured out that Hugh was masquerading as Ralph, nothing was settled, and he saw the strain of it around Louisa's eyes.

Handing her down from the carriage, he escorted her quickly into the inn. Even though they'd been caught in the rain for mere moments, droplets flecked her skin and tugged her curls into darkened strands that hugged her neck.

They stopped at the bottom of the stairs. "I had better change before supper." She tugged off her bonnet and plucked a wet strand of hair from her face, tucking it behind her ear.

Knight nodded curtly, mentally willing himself away from the image of her changing. He followed her upstairs with the intention of changing too but found himself pausing outside of her room. Damn and blast, if he only knew women better, he'd know what to say to ease the strain in her voice and posture.

"I am certain..." He trailed off as she blinked at him expectantly. "That is...we will ensure Hugh does not take the inn. Red will put a stop to it, that much I am certain."

Her lips tilted. "Red is powerful but even he cannot stop a man from claiming what is his."

"It is not his, though."

"No. But it is only my word against his." She wrung her hands together. "I'm glad we found out more about Hugh, but I am worried that it will not be enough to simply *know* it. How do I prove it is not him?"

"We will speak to Abigail. He will not get your inn, I swear it."

Her bottom lip quivered slightly before she set her jaw. "I thank you, Knight. You have been..."

Perhaps it was the vulnerability in her gaze. Maybe it was because she made him so damned weak. Whatever it was, he could fight no longer. He had to comfort this woman somehow and this was the only way he could fathom doing it. He leaned down and pressed his mouth to hers. She gasped, dropped her bonnet, and threw her arms around his neck as she slanted her lips across his.

Fire licked along his insides, burned through his veins. He flattened her back against the door and her fingers scrabbled through his hair.

"Christ." He choked the word out between kisses.

She tasted so damned perfect, felt so damned right. Pushing his fingers under her spencer, he found skin and groaned while she gasped against his mouth.

"Wait."

That whispered word shattered the haze clouding his mind. He froze, a palm to the door, and shoved a hand through his hair.

"Knight, I...." Louisa frowned then skimmed a hand across his face and dropped a kiss onto his chin, then his neck.

The air around them heated again. He glanced down at her, meeting her gaze. With a groan, he flattened her back up against the door and kissed her again. Her mouth opened to his, and he pressed deep. She curled her hands around his shoulders and tried to get closer, her body writhing against his.

Desire ached deep in his gut to the point of pain. He needed this woman more than his next breath. The closing of a door somewhere along the corridor filtered into his mind. He registered that his fingers were gripping her shoulders, that he had her at his mercy, her body soft against his.

He pushed himself back, breaking the kiss with such swiftness that Louisa swayed briefly. She eyed him, her gaze wary and her lips full and red from his kisses. That agonizing desire still needled his gut.

"I cannot do this," he said, voice gruff with need.

"Perhaps..." She drew in a long breath. "Perhaps you should have thought about that before kissing me."

He gave a depreciative laugh. Think? As if he did any thinking around her. If he'd have truly been thinking, he would have kept his distance from the moment he'd first set eyes on her in Penshallow. All those bloody days of lusting after her had done this to him. No damned wonder he could not keep his hands to himself.

"I was trying to comfort you." The words sounded weak and ridiculous when he heard them out loud.

She laughed. "And that is how you comfort a woman? Tease her with kisses then make her look a fool?"

"I had little intention of making you look a fool," he said tightly.

Palms flat against the door at either side of her, she stared up at him. "Why must you deny this?" She shook her head. "You desire me, I know you do."

"It matters not."

Louisa pushed away from the wall and put her hands to her hips. "I'm tired, Knight. Tired of fighting this. Of fighting you."

"Louisa—"

"We are both grown adults with little to hold us back."

"You agreed we would not repeat our previous mistake," he pointed out.

Her cheeks grew red, and she tightened her jaw. "It is clear that neither of us are capable of remembering that. I do not see the harm in two people finding comfort in one another."

"You will find no comfort with me."

"Why are you so insistent of pushing me away?" she demanded. "If you would only talk to me, explain—"

"I do not talk, if you recall. Most know this of me." He winced inwardly at his tone, but he could not have pressed further. This needed to be over, now. And he had to be as far away from her as possible or else he'd drag her back to bed and she'd wake with regret in the morning.

"I know you want me." She curled her fingers around the lapel of his jacket.

The tempting proximity of her sent his pulse racing. Bloody hell, this could not happen. Knight pushed her back, more roughly than he'd intended. She staggered back and gaped at him. He cursed under his breath, fists curled at his sides. The blasted woman was weakening him by the second, but he should never have touched her like that.

"You deserve better than me, Louisa. Even you must be able to see that."

"All I can see, Lewis Knight, is that you are a stubborn fool." Her chest rose and fell with one long breath. "I shall eat in my room tonight. Goodnight."

Before he responded, she scooped up her abandoned bonnet and shoved open the door, slamming it with such force that the wall sconce vibrated, making the candle in the hallway flicker.

Knight exhaled and ran a hand over his face. She might not realize it, but he was right. The more distance between them, the better. Louisa needed someone stable in her life, someone with everything to give. Not some battled-scarred smuggler.

Chapter Twelve

Louisa clenched her eyes tightly shut and tried counting her breaths. One, two, three, four...She huffed. Sleep eluded her while the memory of that kiss surged through her mind over and over. She'd never experienced a kiss like it. How could he push her away after that?

She tossed onto her side and rearranged the tangled bedding around her legs. Her stomach grumbled. Although she had brought dinner up just as she had vowed, she'd been unable to eat much of it and regretted that now. Her stomach had been a jumble of regret and need. If Knight would only talk to her, explain why he was so reticent. But the blasted man was so set on keeping his strong jaw shut she doubted she would ever understand what was going through his mind. She understood that they'd agreed to remain friends but *he* had kissed her.

And she'd seen it—the need in his gaze. It was easily as strong as hers, and he was a fool to deny it. She did not much like being a fool, so she was done fighting it. After all, there were few reasons why they could not give in, and after the day she'd endured, she could think of nothing she wanted more than to be wrapped in his arms.

But, of course, he was insisting on playing the martyr. She thumped a fist against the pillow. Stupid, stupid man.

She stilled and frowned. Something scraped against the door to her room. Drawing her next breath in slowly and silently, she listened carefully. Another scraping sound. Her heart gave a little judder, making her careful breaths harder to draw in. It could not be Knight, she was certain of that. The stubborn man would not give in now.

The door flew open suddenly, crashing against the wall and sending splinters flying across the room. The haze of candlelight illuminated the imposing outlines of several men. Louisa screamed and scrabbled to stand as sheets tangled around bare legs. Three men barged into her room, one coming straight for her. He clamped a hand across her mouth and nose before she could utter a word, making it hard for her to breathe. She lashed out, scratched and kicked at anything within reach. Her toe connected with the bedstead and sent a wave of pain through her. Her cry was muffled against the huge, sweaty palm.

A flash of light catching on a blade sent her heart racing anew. Oh God, they intended to kill her. She clawed at her captor's arms and released his pinching hold over her mouth long enough to draw air. The scent of old sweat fouled her next breath, but the brief reprieve allowed her to scream again and bite down on his hand.

"Bitch."

She hardly saw the movement but she felt it—a blinding light surged across her face when the back of a palm struck her cheek. Knuckles met her cheekbones and the strength in her legs left her. She sagged onto the bed.

Through clouded vision, she spotted the knife once more, looming over her. Louisa slid off the bed, her limbs heavy and her mind thick and muddled. All she knew was that if she did not do something, these men would kill her. She crawled a mere few inches when a rough hand latched around her ankle and forced her to a stop. Groping for something—anything—to protect herself, her fingers met air.

Another man charged into the room, broad shoulders highlighted by the sputtering candlelight of the hallway. The fingers around her ankle released, and she kicked out, even though there was no longer anyone there. When she realized she had her freedom, she huddled into the corner of the room, arms around her knees, away from the fray.

The steady pound in her head continued, but her vision gradually cleared. "Knight!" Relief washed through her.

Knight knocked the knife from one of the men's hands with ease and laid out another with a fist. He grabbed the third and paused. "Bastard," he spat and thrust a punch into his gut. The man retched and collapsed, lying fetal on his side while Knight loomed over him for a moment, drawing in ragged breaths.

Knight rushed over and gripped her arms, aiding her to her feet. "Are you hurt?" He ran hands over her face and her body, and she felt the tremble in them. Or perhaps that was her shaking?

"Tell me you are not hurt."

Louisa shook her head, unable to find any words. Her cheek throbbed and her elbows hurt from when she had rolled off the bed. She had no doubt she would be left with a few bruises from the ordeal. But nothing that would not heal.

She peered around Knight at the three men. Two were knocked senseless while the third remained curled on the floor, coughing and fighting to draw breath. She narrowed her gaze at him.

"Bastard!" Gathering the loose strings at the neck of her nightgown in one hand, she strode over and thrust a finger at him. "You swore on your mother's grave you could tell us nothing more."

Eli Jones groaned and gave a weak smile. "Don't have no mother. Orphan, you see." He sniggered then coughed.

Knight came up behind her. "I should kill him."

"Perhaps you should," Louisa agreed.

Knight raised a brow.

"No, no!" Eli lifted his hands briefly then moaned, wrapping them back around his stomach.

Louisa crouched next to him. "Perhaps I will prevent him from killing you, if you tell me why you tried to hurt me."

"I told Hugh this was a bloody fool's errand, but he don't listen to no one." Eli eased himself up against the wall, an arm banded around his waist. "Hugh was going to send coin if we helped him."

"Help him how?" Louisa pressed.

"Ensure that people still thought he was Ralph." Eli sent Knight a wrathful look. "Of course, he didn't tell us there would be questions asked by someone like you." Eli snorted and looked to Louisa. "He said we'd only have you to deal with and you'd hand over the inn with ease. We couldn't have you going back to Cornwall and telling the truth."

Louisa shared a look with Knight. "It seems you underestimated me, Mr. Jones."

"I don't like killing women," Eli said weakly.

"Whereas I quite enjoy killing men who try to harm women." Knight's stare was cold and sent a shiver even through her. She'd seen the vicious side of Knight before and it was easy to forget that underneath that there was a man with feelings and insecurities. However, she was certain now that there was such a man there.

Louisa rose. "What should we do with them?"

"I shall take care of it." He put an arm around her shoulders and eased her toward the door. "Wait in my room." He handed her the key. "Lock the door and do not open it unless you hear my voice."

She nodded and let him lead her to his room. With one candle lit and the bed untouched, she had to utter up a thank-you that Knight had not been sleeping. "I am glad you heard me."

"I would have heard you even if I was asleep." He shrugged as she peered at him. "A trick I learned in the Army. To go from sleeping to awake at the slightest sound in an instant." He stepped out of the room. "Lock the door, I will not take long."

Louisa dutifully locked the door behind him and sank onto the bed. Arms wrapped around herself, she focused on taking steady breaths and not listening to what was happening in the hallway or a few rooms down. Doors opened and shut and there were voices but she could not make out what was occurring.

She waited in that position until her limbs were stiff. Her heart had slowed but her cheek continued to throb painfully. To think those men had been willing to kill her over the inn. It meant Hugh was more dangerous than simply being a swindler. They would have to move with caution when they revealed who he was.

No. When *she* revealed who he was. Knight had an estate and a title to claim.

A tap on the door made her heart skip back into her throat. "Louisa."

She exhaled and released her arms around from her waist. Barefoot, she padded across the room and unlocked the door. Knight slipped in and locked the door behind him.

"What happened?" she asked, swallowing the knot that seemed to have wedged itself permanently in her throat.

"The innkeeper aided me in clearing them out and sending someone to fetch the local constable."

She nodded. The thought of them locked up made the tightness in her chest ease.

"The innkeeper shall ensure they see justice. He can press charges for them entering his property." He glanced her over. "You are cold."

Until he hauled his jacket off the back of a chair and slung it across her shoulders, she had little idea of what he meant. When the warmth surrounded her, tinged with the scent of soap and musk, she finally noted she'd been shivering. She huddled into the heavy wool gratefully and forced a smile.

"I suppose we had—"

A hand to her cheek trapped the words in her throat. He skimmed a finger down her face, his expression grim.

"If I had been with you, this never would have happened."

He stepped away before she responded and dipped a cloth in the washbowl atop a slim washstand. Knight wrung out the water and urged her to sit on the bed. With the sort of tenderness she would expect from someone half Knight's size, he dabbed her cheek then pressed the cloth to the swelling. She sucked in a breath as the cool fabric met the heat in her face.

Meeting his gaze, she curled her fingers around his wrist and lowered his hand. "Knight, I—"

"Forgive me," he murmured and leaned in to kiss her.

She had no time to decide whether he meant for what had just happened or whether he was apologizing for the kiss. Either way, he needed no forgiveness, but she found herself unable to say as much when he moved his mouth to her swollen cheek and dropped a tender kiss there, then one on the bridge of her nose and another to her forehead.

Louisa closed her eyes and absorbed his tenderness. Rain pattered gently against the window and the bed creaked as he cupped a hand behind her head and eased her onto it. She coiled her arms around his neck, clinging like a sailor to a shipwreck. The feel of him, strong and secure against her body, made her mind swirl.

He kissed her lips again, and she opened her eyes to view him while she pushed her fingers through the soft strands of his dark hair then brought them down to cup his bristled jaw. An unbidden smile curved her lips. The candlelight warmed one side of his face, casting the other side in shadow. His gaze searched hers, a question lingering there. He might be a man of few words but she knew what he wanted.

"Please do not deny me again," she pleaded.

Knight grunted. "As if I could."

He touched a finger to her lips and she parted them, drawing in a breath thickened by need. Hitching up her chemise, he eased her legs apart and let his fingers linger on her thigh. She clutched him tight while his hand trailed up to her center, and she rose up to meet his touch.

"Oh." She closed her eyes and tilted her head back while his fingers danced over her, sending delicious whorls of pleasure through her. He kissed her neck and drew her lobe between his teeth, making her shudder.

The sheets rustled beneath them while he freed himself from his breeches. Opening her eyes, Louisa lifted her head to meet his kiss and drew him fully onto her. His gaze latched onto hers as he joined them, inch by inch, moment by moment. She gasped at the sensation and felt the heat of tears in the corner of her eyes. He rocked into her, and she buried her head against his chest until the pleasure broke and washed over them both.

Knight said nothing as he tugged the blankets over them both and took her in his arms. Louisa smiled to herself. Of course she expected no different from him, but at least he was not running away from her this time.

Chapter Thirteen

Splinters of daylight seeped through the shutters, dusting Louisa's bare skin with an ethereal glow. Knight swallowed and ran his gaze over her. A bruise stained her cheek and several scratches were visible. If he'd only reached her sooner, she would never have suffered so.

He lifted a hand and let it hover over her shoulder. The heat of her body seeped through the gap, beckoning to him. There was nothing he wanted more than to wake her with kisses and take her again. But reason fled him when he was lost in her. He could not let it happen again. He'd already spilled in her once and if she caught, he would be honor bound to marry her. That was something neither of them wanted—even if she did not realize it yet. He was hardly suited to the role of husband let alone father.

Knight gave in, briefly. He lowered the hand and stroked the bare skin of her shoulder. She began to rouse, her lids fluttered as she rolled onto her back. Standing swiftly, he sought out his breeches and tugged them on. The cut on his back sent a swift spear of pain through him, and he winced. Apparently brawling last night had done damage again, and he suspected he'd re-opened the wound.

Louisa stretched and peered blearily up at him. "What time is it?"

He struggled to answer for a moment. With her hair tousled around her shoulders, the sheets caressing her naked body, and her lips rosy and swollen, she was temptation in itself.

"Knight?" she prompted.

"Right. Yes." He twisted and fished his pocket watch from his jacket, flipping it open and grimacing. "Nearly midday."

"I cannot recall the last time I slept so late." She gave a small smile.

"We had better make haste if we are to speak to Mrs. Stanton."

She nodded, opened her mouth then closed it again.

"Louisa, I—"

Her lips curved. "You know, you rarely use my name."

No. It was too dangerous. Her name on his lips made him feel weak. Hell, *she* made him feel weak.

"How are you feeling?" he asked, his voice low while he silently cursed himself for his cowardice. All he needed to do was remind her of who he was—*what* he was. She had an inn and a life to return home to and had no need of a man like him.

"A little sore." She chewed on her bottom lip before lifting her gaze to his. "Knight..."

"We cannot let that happen again," he said swiftly. If he waited any longer, he was going to wind up bedding her again and getting lost in her sweet kisses and even sweeter body.

Something flickered in her gaze, and she drew up her knees, wrapping her arms about the sheets covering them. She nodded slowly. "I know."

He released a long exhale. She agreed. That was what he wanted.

Why then did it stab at his gut to know she thought it a mistake too?

"I am a smuggler, Louisa." Her name slipped from his lips, and he regretted it. It tasted too good on his tongue, made him want to climb back under the sheets with her and say it over and over, letting the words caress her skin. "My life is dangerous...and complicated. I know you do not need such a person in your life."

She lifted her gaze to his. "I understand, Knight. You need not defend yourself." She reached out to him, and he found himself closing the distance between them and placing his hand in hers. When she curled her fingers around his large hand, he had to drag his gaze away from the sight. "I do not regret last night, but you are right—we cannot let that happen again."

He forced himself to swallow the knot in his throat. "Good." The word came out strained.

"Besides, you are not only a smuggler, you are a viscount."

"Most women would think that an advantage."

"I am not most women, and a simple innkeeper cannot marry...that is..." Louisa clamped her mouth shut.

He nodded and blew out a breath thick with frustration. This was the response he needed. If they both vowed that they would not repeat this, there would be no temptation. He should not be frustrated, but he damn well was. He eased his hand from her grip then scooped up his shirt and wrenched it over his head, thrusting his arms violently into the sleeves and pulling it down. Aware of her gaze on him, he purposely avoided looking at her while he shoved his feet into boots and left the laces un-done.

"I shall fetch some food while you ready yourself," he told her. "Then we can go to Abigail's lodgings."

"Thank you," she murmured.

"You have nothing to thank me for."

"You saved me last night. And have delayed your plans for several days. Not to mention..." She gave a strained smile. "Well, you comforted me when I needed it most."

Uncertain how to respond, he simply gave a curt nod and left the room. He could have requested food for them and been served fairly rapidly. Despite the time of day, the taproom was not even half-full. He imagined a lot of the guests had travelled on and new ones would not arrive until the evening. However, he waited to order food until he had drained an ale. The cold liquid flowed through him, and he closed his eyes to savor it. If he had nothing better to do, he would be tempted to indulge in several more in an attempt to silence his own rambling thoughts, but Louisa was waiting on him.

With any luck, they would persuade Abigail to return to Cornwall with Louisa and identify Hugh as her husband. Once that was done, he would leave for Northumberland immediately and settle this damned estate business. By the time he returned, their nights together would be forgotten and he could go back to the stasis that was him watching her from afar.

And his gritty life as a smuggler, ducking the excise men and using his brawn and jagged looks to intimidate any who thought to cross them.

Knight returned to the room to find Louisa dressed with her hair tied up in a ribbon. He offered her a plate of fish and sliced meat, and he eased himself down onto the chair in the corner while she remained on the bed. They ate in silence, and he could not claim to have tasted one morsel of it. Temptation kept pulling its tantalizing lasso, drawing his gaze to her. Fingers tight around his fork, he eyed the bruise on her cheek. Anger ran its hot, spikey fingers through him until he let his gaze fall on her lips or her neck, even the wispy curls surrounding her face. Then he was transported back to last night. He could not fail to recall every soft moment, every whispered word. He'd never made love to a woman before—not truly.

As much as he tried to fight this, there was no denying this was not some primitive attraction. Though that only meant he had to fight harder. He would not hurt Louisa for all the world.

He finished his food and took Louisa's empty plate to stack them on the side table. "We should head to Mrs. Stanton's."

Nodding, she stood and straightened her skirts. "The sooner we prove this man is not who he says he is, the better."

"Then what shall you do with him?"

She stilled, a hand halfway to smoothing her hair back. A crinkle appeared between her brows. "I had not thought that through really. I would have said simply send him away but after last night..."

"If he put his friends up to that, he deserves to see justice," Knight said, grimly.

"But Abigail..."

He lifted a shoulder. Abigail needed someone better than that man in her life, but he knew it was not as easy as that. His mother might have left his father years ago if she was not utterly dependent on him. He might have mourned her death after Julianna was born, but he'd been relieved she'd been able to escape him in a way—and somehow it had guilted his father into behaving in a relatively decent manner with Julianna.

"Let us persuade her she must reveal him for who he is first," he suggested. "Then we can worry what to do about him."

The carriage awaited them at the front of the tavern, causing a few angry shouts and curses as it blocked one side of the road. The driver waved the irate people on with a dismissive hand while one of the footmen opened the door. Knight would look forward to being rid of this carriage too. He had every intention of sending Louisa and Abigail back in it. They would arrive home safely and with haste. As much as he wanted to get this business with the family estate settled, he would take the delays that would come with travelling with mail coaches and shared transport so long as Louisa was safe.

He would not miss the pomp that came with a private carriage either. He didn't know how Red did it all the time.

Louisa tapped her fingers against the window ledge. He rested his hands on his thighs and bunched his muscles to avoid the temptation to lean over and curl a hand over her fingers. She hadn't said much about the men who tried to hurt her, and knowing Louisa, she would dismiss any comforting words he could manage. He still felt he had to try, however.

Knight unfurled a hand and lifted it, flattening it hesitantly on her shoulder. Clearly lost in thought, she jumped, and he withdrew his hand quickly.

"Forgive me."

She shook her head. "No, sorry. I was just thinking..."

"I only wanted to say...that is...you were brave indeed last night."

Her lips curved. "Thank you, Knight."

"You're, um, welcome." He snapped his attention to outside. Curses. What a damned fool he must sound. He should never try to comfort a woman ever again.

The busy roads ensured their journey lasted for more uncomfortable minutes than he wanted, but he noted Louisa's fidgeting had ceased and the concerned expression puckering her brow relaxed.

The driver pulled the carriage to a halt where they'd stopped previously, and they made their way through the tight alleys, Knight leading the way with ease now they knew where they were going. He paused when the house came into sight, and Louisa stumbled into him.

"What..." Her words died as she peered around him.

The door to Mrs. Stanton's house was open, hanging from its hinges. Wood splinters revealed exactly how it was forced open and the boot print marring the flecked paint was sizeable.

"Oh no." A hand to her mouth, Louisa shook her head slowly. "Oh no," she repeated.

Knight inhaled slowly. Apparently Louisa had not been the only one attacked last night.

Chapter Fourteen

Dried wax clung to the wall sconce in ugly white rivulets. It must have been left burning unattended for a while. What few belongings Abigail possessed were spilled across the gloomy room—the straw mattress tossed over and sheets strewn everywhere. The bassinet from the corner of the room was gone and a storage box lay upside down, cracked.

Nausea rose in Louisa's throat. Her room had looked similar after Eli and his men attacked her. Had the same thing happened to Abigail and the children? She cast a glance at Knight's grim expression. He met her gaze, and she could see the answer—something terrible had happened to them.

"What sort of person would hurt children?" She moved to stand in the center of the squalid room and eyed the desolation.

"The sort who would hurt a woman," Knight said, his jaw tight.

A hand to her mouth, she surveyed the room again, as though she might spot something that would tell her otherwise—that the children and Abigail were safe and had simply left for the day.

"I'll go and find out if anyone saw anything." Knight ducked out of the building, leaving the door ajar.

Strips of leaden-tinged daylight highlighted the devastation. A splintered chair sat abandoned on the floor as though it had been thrown against the wall in a fit of anger. Wind whistled down the chimney into the empty fireplace. She wrapped her arms about herself and shuddered. Oh Lord, what had she done? She'd brought this upon Abigail.

A hand to her arm made her whirl, a fist raised. She dropped it and sagged. "Forgive me."

Knight shook his head and frowned. "You are upset."

"Of course." Her voice wavered slightly. "Are you not?"

"Yes, but..." His frown deepened. He reached up and swiped a tear from her cheek, leaving a cool patch on her skin.

She sniffed and swiped a hand across her eyes. "I did this." She motioned to the barren room.

"Eli and his friends did this."

"No, what I mean is...this is my fault. If I had not started asking questions, if I had stayed put in Cornwall..." She drew in a breath. None of it would have happened. Including bedding Knight.

And somehow she could not bring herself to regret that even though she had not lied when she had said they should not let it happen again. As much as she'd been frustrated by his reticence in the heat of the moment, the morning light had brought clarity and reminded her of all the reasons they should not be risking such behavior.

Especially when her heart began to ache every time she was near him. He made it clear he had no interest in having a woman in his life, and she would have to remember that.

"If you had stayed in Cornwall, we would not have found out about Hugh's ruse, and you would lose the inn." He took her arms in his hands, forcing her gaze to his. "This is all Hugh's doing. Not yours, Louisa."

There it was again. Her name on his lips, soft but penetrating, like cupid's arrow aimed straight for her heart—piercing but with benevolent intentions. Her heart gave a little flutter as she looked into those deep, dark eyes. She glanced away before she gave anything away. They'd vowed to forget it a mere hour or so ago. She could not reveal she was weakening already.

She gulped past the tightening in her throat. "Did anyone see anything?"

He shook his head and removed his hat, tucking it under his arm and shoving a hand through his dark hair. Louisa fought to prevent herself from watching the display, recalling how those thick strands had felt between her fingers.

"Have you looked around?" he asked. "Seen if there is anything to tell us where she went?"

"No," she admitted. She'd been too wrapped up in her guilt to think of doing something useful. What clues could there possibly be in this small dwelling, though? She rotated, surveying every inch of the room and frowned. "If this was Eli and his accomplices, why would they have come for me?"

Knight's expression eased. "Abigail and the children must have escaped unharmed or else they would not have needed to come for you. Abigail is the one who can identify Hugh."

A wave of relief washed over her, making her sag. She dropped onto the one unharmed chair and rested her chin on a hand. "Thank goodness. But where could they have gone?"

He lifted a shoulder. "No one could tell me much of her. No family in the area it seems."

A piece of paper crumpled up in the fire place caught Louisa's eye. She narrowed her gaze and rose to look closer. Plucking it up, she unfolded it. The writing was poor and smudged, as though written in haste. Knight peered over her shoulder.

"Abigail cannot have written this surely?" Not many women of her status could write. Louisa had been lucky that her father had insisted on teaching her before she worked on their farm, insisting that she would do better for herself. She tilted her head and eyed the words. "It makes no sense, either. But look—" She jabbed at the letter "—my name."

"It's in code."

Louisa twisted to view Knight, her heart jolting at his nearness. "Code?"

He nodded and took the letter from her. "We used it in France. Perhaps Abigail learned it from Hugh if he served, though few foot soldiers acquired the skill." He smirked. "I was a mere extra body, but I could read and write so I was tasked with communications at times."

She opened her mouth and closed it. The life Knight had led before coming to Cornwall was full of tragic stories, she was certain of it. Drake—who was injured in battle—still suffered because of his experiences at times, according to Julianna. She had no doubt Knight had endured similar moments. If only he would open up to her about them.

Oh Lord, what was she thinking? This was Knight. He opened up to no one. She needed to cease these foolish wanderings of her mind and concentrate on the problem at hand.

"Can you decipher it? Is it from Abigail?" she pressed.

He ran his gaze over the letter a few times, his mouth moving silently with the words. "She sought shelter outside of town. A farmhouse four miles east, it says." He lifted his gaze to hers. "She must have known they were coming for her."

Louisa pressed a hand to her stomach. How did Abigail make it four miles with all those young children in the dead of night? Would they have arrived unmolested? Oh dear, if only they'd stayed with her or persuaded her to come with them or—

"There was nothing you could do. You could not have predicted this."

She snapped her gaze up to his. How on earth did he read her so easily?

"I just wish..." She sighed. "I do not know, but I wish none of this had ever happened."

Knight's expression shuttered just as a flash of hurt creased his face. She cursed herself inwardly. That wasn't what she had meant. Perhaps nothing should have ever happened between them, but she could not bring herself to wish it away.

"Knight..." She put a hand to his arm.

"We had better make haste. We need to ensure Abigail and the children are safe." He folded the letter and tucked it into his breast pocket then put his hat back on.

"Of course." Louisa straightened her shoulders and followed him out of the building, drawing the lopsided door shut behind her.

Knight directed the carriage driver to head east out of the town but vehicles clogged the streets, slowing their progress into the countryside. Louisa pressed a breath through her nose and twined her hands together. When she got her hands on Hugh...

"There's a farmhouse. That must be it."

Louisa looked in the direction to which Knight pointed. A ramshackle farmhouse broke the empty fields, its red brick a stark contrast to the yellowed fields around it. White sash windows peered out at the surrounding land and Louisa heard a dog barking as they neared.

Knight rapped his knuckles on the roof and the carriage rolled to a stop. Louisa had to force herself to disembark slowly from the vehicle. Lord, she prayed Abigail and the children were safe. She'd never forgive herself if she'd muddled them up in this and brought harm upon them.

A large scruffy dog with a coat of gray and pale-yellow streaks bounded up to Knight, barking. Knight paused and eyed the animal. Louisa grimaced. No doubt the animal saw Knight as a threat given his size.

"Here, doggy," she called softly in a bid to distract him.

Knight tried to take a step forward but the dog shadowed him, preventing him from moving. Shaking his head, Knight dropped slowly to a crouch and offered out his hand. She could not make out what he was saying, but he murmured something to the animal.

"Perhaps I should—" Louisa paused when she noticed the dog had ceased barking. She cocked her head and observed as the dog slowly approached Knight, giving his fingers a tentative sniff then a lick. Knight scratched the animal's head and the dog leaned into his hand.

"You are good with animals," she murmured, unable to keep the astonishment out of her voice.

Knight shrugged his great shoulders. "We had dogs on my father's estate." He rose slowly and the dog lost interest and headed back to the house. "He is only doing his duty and protecting his property."

The front door opened before they reached it and a short lady with a white frilly cap tied around her head stepped out. Before she could say anything, a man barreled up to them from the courtyard, a rifle in hand.

Chapter Fifteen

"**G**et away or I'll shoot," the man warned.

Knight peered down at the farmer and the gun clasped in trembling hands. He doubted the man was quaking with nerves—he was tall, a little thin, but strong from farm work, and seething with anger. His cheeks were red, his nostrils flaring. If it were just Knight, he would not be so concerned. After all, he'd taken many a rifle shot and lived. However, he was not willing to put Louisa in danger. Knight lifted both palms in surrender.

"Oh, Samuel, put the gun down!" The woman hastened over, flapping a handkerchief in her hand at the farmer. "Abigail says they are friends."

Knight peered around the man and the barrel pointing at his gut to spy Abigail in the doorway of the farmhouse with the baby in her arms.

"Oh thank goodness," Louisa exclaimed. "She's safe."

"We are not, though," Knight muttered.

"Samuel, lower the gun!" the older woman insisted. "I will not have you shooting anyone in front of the children."

The man lifted a thick gray brow and eyed Knight up and down. "Are you certain these are her friends, Barbara?"

"Yes, yes." The woman fluttered her hands at him. "Put down the gun!"

Louisa took a step forward and the farmer shifted his gun toward her. Knight had to force himself to remain still lest the farmer mistake a sudden movement as a threat but, damn, it took every ounce of his willpower not to jump between her and that long barrel aimed directly at her heart.

"We are her friends," Louisa insisted, her tone placatory. "We came to ensure she and the children were safe. The men who threatened her also threatened me."

Samuel narrowed his gaze and a few heavy heartbeats passed. He finally nodded and lowered the barrel. "Never can be too careful."

"I am glad someone so diligent in looking after Abigail. Please, can we speak with her?" Louisa asked.

"She is mighty shaken," Barbara explained. "And you say those men tried to harm you? Oh you poor thing, you must have been terrified too."

"I am well enough," Louisa said with a smile.

Barbara smiled. "I imagine your husband here ensured they did not set a hand on you. Unfortunately that useless husband of Mrs. Stanton's had vanished, leaving her all alone and defenseless."

"I can defend her," Samuel said with a grunt.

"Yes, we know, dear." Barbara waved a dismissive hand. "You are strong and are as good an aim as you always were." Barbara took Louisa's arm. "Will you not come in? The fire is lit, and I have just warmed a kettle."

Louisa nodded gratefully and allowed herself to be led into the house. The dog on their heels, Knight and Samuel followed after them.

"Sorry for the welcome." Samuel glanced at Knight. "My wife tasked me with keeping Mrs. Stanton safe, and she would have my neck if I let her get hurt. Besides, she's a good girl and doesn't deserve this rotten situation." The man shook his head. "Who threatens women and children anyway?"

Knight ignored the apology. It was not the first time he'd been threatened with a gun and it would not be the last. Unfortunately his size and face attracted trouble.

"The men behind this have been locked up for now. The innkeeper where we are staying will press charges and ensure they are punished," Knight told him.

"Ah, indeed. So they caused more trouble, did they?" Samuel shook his head. "What a sorry state of affairs."

Barbara led them into a wide kitchen with low beams that forced Knight to angle his head. True to her word, a fire crackled in the grate and the scent of wood smoke wrapped about the room. A generous dining table occupied the center of the room. Several of the children could be heard running about one of the other rooms while the baby slept peacefully in Abigail's arms. Abigail herself appeared tired but unharmed.

"Will you not sit?" Barbara invited. "Did I hear it right that these men have been apprehended?"

"Is it true?" Abigail asked.

Knight nodded as Louisa sat. "They broke into Louisa's room and tried to harm her. They have been apprehended and will face punishment." Knight sank gratefully onto one of the chairs and rubbed the slight ache from his neck. "Did they try to harm you?"

Abigail eased onto a chair as well while Barbara busied herself pouring what smelled to be strong coffee into mugs for them all. Samuel kept a watchful eye over the proceedings, his gun resting in his arms much like Abigail's baby rested in hers.

"I overheard a conversation when I went to draw water. There was concern I was going to reveal that Hugh is not really your stepson. I gathered up the children and we came here." Abigail smiled up at the farmer's wife. "Mrs. Blackmore brings food to the church for the poor so I knew I could count on her charity."

Louisa cupped her hand around one of the mugs of coffee. "Thank goodness she had you, Mrs. Blackmore."

Barbara's cheeks reddened, and she waved the cloth in her hand. "Oh, shush. I was only doing what any good Christian woman would do."

Knight peered at Abigail. "Did you leave the letter for us?"

She nodded. "I was not certain you would come back, but I suspected you needed me after overhearing their conversation."

"Where did you learn to write in code?" he enquired.

Abigail looked down at the table. "I was a nurse in France before I married Hugh. That was how we met, I tended to him after he was injured in battle." Her smile turned sad. "I had a knack for writing so one of the officers taught me so I could aid with communications. I knew no one else would be able to read it, but you are a military man, are you not?"

Knight supposed all the scars were evidence in itself, but he could not help be surprised by Abigail's intelligence. How did someone like her end up desolate and poor with a bastard for a husband? She was clearly an innocent in all of this.

Knight nodded in response.

"Eli admitted they were to help pretend Hugh is my stepson," Louisa explained. "If anyone asked about him, they were to cover for him."

Abigail's expression dropped. "So he really was not planning on returning for us."

No one said anything. Knight shifted in his chair.

"You know, Hugh received a letter not long ago." Abigail's brow puckered. "He asked the vicar to read it for him and seemed terribly excited. I didn't understand why he did not ask me, but when I asked about it, he got angry, so I didn't ask about it again. It was then that his behavior changed completely. He kept sneaking away." She grimaced. "I thought he was whoring but perhaps it was something to do with your stepson."

Louisa looked Knight's way. "Perhaps there was some sort of confusion at the war office. Did you know my stepson during your time as a nurse?"

Abigail shook her head. "Hugh mentioned him. He said he was missing and presumed dead in the same battle in which Hugh was harmed. Hugh was known to be his friend so maybe they sent whatever it was to him in the hopes he might pass it on to Ralph's family."

Knight nodded. "That sounds a reasonable assumption."

The baby in Abigail's arms began to rouse. She looked down at the baby then at Knight, her brow creased with worry. "What do I do now?"

"You could confront him," Knight suggested.

Louisa rolled her eyes. "What Knight means, is we need to reveal his ruse. We cannot let him get away with this."

Abigail bit down on her bottom lip. "I-I'm not sure I can. He *is* my husband."

"If he were my husband," said Barbara, "he'd suffer a lot more than a mere confrontation."

Samuel nodded and chuckled. "Don't I know it. He's left you and the babies to fend for yourselves, Mrs. Stanton. And if what you tell us is correct, he intends to take this woman's livelihood."

Abigail released her bottom lip and sighed. "I will help you. I feel awful. I should have known what he was doing."

"You are not the keeper of your husband, Abigail," Louisa assured her. "If you can help me ensure his claim to my inn is rejected, I will do whatever I can to make sure you and the children are looked after."

Knight could not help but smile to himself. Louisa could be hard-nosed when she wanted but she loved to take in waifs and strays, including his sister. Though he had offered to aid Julianna when he discovered she was in Cornwall, she'd insisted on looking after herself, and Louisa had been instrumental in ensuring his sister had a place to live and an honest wage.

"When do we leave?" Abigail asked. "And what on earth do I do with all the children?"

"We can take the older ones," suggested Barbara. "Can we not, Samuel?" She looked to her husband, who quickly hid his panicked expression.

"Oh yes, yes, of course. Just until your business is completed." He gave a tense smile.

Knight leaned into Louisa. "If you take the carriage home and accompany Abigail, you can have this settled promptly."

Louisa considered this for a moment and shook her head slowly. "I'm coming with you."

"No." He uttered the single syllable before he had quite registered what she had said.

"I'm accompanying you to Northumberland. Your wound is not yet healed. I saw you wincing this morning."

"No," he repeated.

"You need someone to tend to it and ensure you do not injure yourself further." She set her jaw, and Knight grimaced.

"No."

"You can try to force me into the carriage but you will not succeed."

"You are injured, Mr. Knight?" Abigail asked. "Was it those men?"

"No." God, he seemed to be saying that a lot recently.

"But he had to fight them off yesterday, and I think he opened up the wound," Louisa told Mrs. Stanton as if he were not there.

"It could get infected," Abigail mused.

"Precisely." Louisa thrust a finger at him. "I am not having you dying of infection. I shall never forgive myself."

Knight swung his gaze between the two women and lifted a brow. How on earth did he find himself in such a situation? Being bullied by two petite women who had far more pressing things to worry about?

"You are meant to return home," Knight reminded Louisa in undertones. "There was a deadline remember."

She leaned into him. "He is not who he says he is. I can prove that at any time. And Abigail will be safe in Red's carriage. If you write to Red, I am certain he will ensure she and the little ones are looked after."

Damn. Her logic was impeccable. And his wound hurt like the devil. He doubted he'd drop dead from a small slice but it was in such a position that he'd have a hell of a time cleaning it on the almost week-long journey to Northumberland.

He met Samuel's gaze, who just gave an amused shrug. Even he would not argue with these stubborn women.

"Fine. You can accompany me."

Her triumphant grin had his stomach sinking. It was going to be even harder to keep distance between them once they returned to his home. He could only hope his business would be settled quickly and Louisa did not attempt to pry into his past. Knowing the persistent woman, he doubted he'd be lucky enough for that to happen, however.

Chapter Sixteen

Twining her hands in her lap, Louisa kept her gaze fixed on the passing countryside. She chuckled to herself. The carriage moved swiftly along roads that were dry compared to those in Bristol. It seemed it had not rained in this part of the country.

She caught Knight frowning at her. "What's wrong?"

"I was wondering what amused you." He looked a little sheepish as though he had not wanted to be caught watching her.

"I was just thinking that I could have grown used to riding in the earl's carriage." She smiled. "I have turned into a pampered lady already."

"Unfortunately hired coaches are not nearly so comfortable as Red's."

She nodded and tried not to recall the aches in her muscles. Beneath her, the seat was hardly padded, and every time she rested back, she was jolted about thanks to the carriage not being nearly so new or well-sprung as Red's. As a result, she was forced to keep herself upright and her muscles were aching from the exertion.

"We will have to change carriages at Nottingham." He hefted out an audible breath. "You would be more comfortable resting against me." The suggestion stumbled out of his mouth reluctantly.

Louisa hesitated. They had been on the road several hours and having so much time to dwell on things meant the memories of their night together were still fresh—too fresh. She was not sure she trusted herself to be in his arms again.

She winced when they hit a rut and was knocked into the side of the carriage. Knight offered a hand. "I will not do anything untoward, if that is your concern."

Giving him a tilted smile, she took his hand and settled next to him, allowing him to wrap an arm around her shoulders and act as a cradle against the jarring movement of the vehicle. For all of Knight's rough moments, he had never been anything but a gentleman toward her.

"I hope Abigail will be well," she murmured.

"The driver and footmen will ensure she is, and I have left specific instructions with them to give to Red. He will make sure she and the children are safe."

Louisa grimaced at the memory of packing Abigail and her three youngest children into the carriage. Perhaps she should have gone with them, but how could she leave Knight after all he had done for her?

She mused on Knight's comments. Red was no ordinary earl. That mere fact he insisted on being called by his nickname rather than his title was something. He'd never used his station for anything other than good, and Louisa had always appreciated that about him.

"How did you meet Red? He's never said." She peered up at him.

His body tensed briefly then released in what she supposed was surrender. "I stole from him."

Louisa blinked. "You stole?"

He nodded. "I was working with...some rather unsavory men in London. I helped take some stuff from one of his ships. Red tracked me down somehow and was impressed with my skills, so offered me work."

"That was after you left the Army?"

His body tightened again. "Yes."

"Why—?"

"You should have returned home," he said sharply, cutting her off.

Drawing in a lengthy breath, she felt her cheeks heat at the obvious chastisement. "I was not trying to pry."

"Could have fooled me," he muttered.

She tried to pull out of his arms, but he did not let her, holding her effectively captive. "Knight, let me go," she protested.

"Damn it, Louisa, any fool could see you were uncomfortable sitting there." He relaxed his hold on her slightly. "I just...I do not wish to speak of the war, that is all."

Louisa relented, easing back into his hold and staring at the frayed fabric of the chair opposite. She understood him not wanting to speak of the experience, really she did, but silly fool that she was, she'd thought he might trust her enough to open up a little.

They drove past a small farmhouse and a cluster of estate buildings. A grand house could be seen on the horizon, past a thick length of tall trees. It was hard to imagine Knight living in such a house, even as a young man, let alone owning one. Returning home after such a long time would be hard for him, no matter what he said, so she ought to be patient with him. After all, he'd helped her out enormously. She stared at her hands. Without him, she might have been killed.

"What is the matter?"

His voice rumbled in his chest, vibrating through her in a strangely comforting way.

She kept her gaze on her hands. "I was just thinking how close I came to losing the inn." She inhaled. "I do not know what I would do without it."

"You have done well to run such an establishment alone."

She curved her lips. "My husband did not think I was up to the task."

"Your husband did not know you."

She snapped her gaze up to find him looking down at her. "Because of my youth, he did not always believe me capable. Even when his health began to fail and I took charge of it, I knew he wished Ralph were alive to take it over." Her throat tightened.

"A man expects to pass things on to his son. I do not believe that was a judgement on your abilities."

"No, I suppose not. Though, your father did not wish to pass anything on to you, did he?"

"My father was a sadistic bastard." His lips twisted. "He took pleasure in cutting me off with little care as to his legacy. He cared only about himself."

"What of your legacy? Do you not wish to save it?"

"And do what with it?" He grunted. "I have no sons to pass anything on to and an estate without money is no good to anyone. I will sell anything I can to settle my father's inevitable debts and rent it out, and good riddance to it."

Louisa frowned. "Surely his debts cannot be that great?"

He smirked. "They were already huge when I left. I think cutting me off was one of his ways of saving money for himself. Anything other than what was entailed to me will be long gone, and he's had plenty of years to accrue more. You would be surprised what a lavish lifestyle can cost."

"I am sorry he treated you so poorly."

He shrugged. "My only regret was leaving Julianna behind. He treated her well usually. I never thought he would sell her into a marriage."

"Well, you put a stop to that."

"With the help of Drake." He added that with a scowl.

Though Knight had accepted the marriage between the flirtatious captain and his sister, especially after Drake had saved Julianna's life, she supposed there were not many men who would want their sisters married to such a rake. However, Drake was a devoted husband and could give Knight little cause for complaint now.

"They have a good marriage and at least she is happy now," she said wistfully.

Sometimes it seemed as though there were happy couples all around her. As busy as she was, it was hard not to notice that the three founding members of Red's crew were married now.

"Yes, he is a good husband," he admitted, reluctance edging his voice. "Was your...that is, did Jack treat you well?"

"Jack was a good husband—well as good as I could expect. He was much older than me but a decent man. He wanted a wife

to aid him in the running of the inn, and I needed a husband."
She lifted her shoulders. "There is not much more to tell."

"So you did not, er, love him?"

She shook her head. "I was fond of him. It was about as much as I could expect. I cannot complain too much. I did end up with the inn, after all."

The carriage halted abruptly, sending Louisa rocking forward. Knight grabbed her, wrapping an arm about her front like a shield. The feel of his muscled arm against her breasts sent heat whirling through her body, and she remembered gripping those arms all too well.

She tucked a strand of hair behind her ear and noticed his jaw working. "Thank you."

He nodded before thrusting his head out of the window. "Just got to water the horses," she heard the driver say.

"Do you wish to stretch your legs?" he asked Louisa.

"Yes." She stretched and winced. "Make that certainly yes."

They disembarked the carriage, and Knight pressed a hand to his back. Louisa eyed him, and he removed his hand hastily. No doubt all this travelling was taking a toll on his body too but the stubborn man would never admit as much.

"Should I take a look at your wound?"

He waved a hand. "It is well enough." He spotted her raised brow and added, "Besides, there is little you can do here."

Louisa paused to eye the countryside. The horses refreshed themselves from a water trough sitting in front of a mile-marker so she could not make out where they were. Not that it mattered. She knew even less about this part of the country than she did Bristol, but the countryside was wild, tinged with yellows and purples and extravagantly beautiful. All it needed was a touch of ocean and she'd almost feel as though she was home.

She strolled along the road toward the steep edge of the hill that sliced down into the rock and overlooked a shallow valley. Wind whipped through the curls around her face and she shoved them back, aware of Knight's gaze fixed upon her. He had yet to move from where he had disembarked and yet she could sense him, even if she did not look at him.

Blowing out a breath, she wrapped her arms about herself and shut her eyes, tilting her head to clear skies. Sun danced over her face, casting shadows behind her closed lids. The fresh air filled her lungs, and she let the sensation wash over her until her neck prickled. She opened her eyes and turned to find Knight closer now. He shifted his gaze swiftly, but she caught it in his gaze—the longing.

That same longing she felt. And as much as she'd like to tell herself she'd only come here to tend to this wound, there was more to it than that.

Stupidly, foolishly, she hoped for more. More moments together. Another mistaken night perhaps. Even if it led to nothing.

Chapter Seventeen

Out of the corner of his eye, he saw Louisa's mouth drop open. He fixed his gaze on the carriage interior behind her. His heart pounded hard in his chest, but he could not bring himself to look at the approach to the house.

His house.

It had been a long, long time, but it would be the same. The long road lined with old oak trees, the thick columns, the tall sash windows, the generous stables to the side that had been built out of the same stone as the house when his father expanded the building to fit in a new ballroom and drawing rooms.

Nothing had changed and nothing would change. Once everything was settled, he would return to what he did best—skirting on the edge of the law and using his brawn for whatever was needed.

"It's beautiful, Knight," Louisa breathed.

He could not help himself. He leaned to peer out of the window to watch the approach. Just as he'd thought, it was all the same with the exception of a new fountain in front of the house, which had likely cost a sizeable fortune. It was not running today and apparently no one had noticed his approach as there were no servants waiting to greet him. Not that he anticipated anyone cared much, but he knew his father always expected as much from the staff.

"I will deal with this business as quickly as possible. Most of it can be managed by letter, but I will need to speak with my father's lawyer. Then we can return home and ensure Ralph is sent on his way."

She nodded but kept her gaze on the house. "If this were mine...Gosh, I do not know how I would part with it."

Knight twisted his lips. "With ease. You would take one look at the cost of maintaining it and flee."

She chuckled. "I suppose the staff wages alone are outrageous."

"Indeed." And no wonder there was no one waiting to greet him. They likely knew they would all be out of a job before long unless the new tenants decided to keep them on. He would have to do his best to secure the jobs that he could.

A heavy weight sat in his stomach as the carriage eased to a halt in front of the house. The façade loomed over him, austere and commanding, much like his father had been. Knight's size had been the one thing he'd had in common with his father, and his father used it to full advantage, frequently threatening anyone who dare dissatisfy him—including Knight. Finally reaching the same height as his father had been gratifying, but it had taken some time for him to finally stand up to the man.

As Knight opened the door, a man stepped out of the house and remained waiting on the plinth in front of the house. Knight ducked out of the vehicle and aided Louisa down before viewing the servants.

Posture stiff, his gaze unflinching, the butler eyed them both while they approached the house. Knight took in a long breath. The last time he'd seen Hayward, had been when he'd left for good. It was hard to believe the man was still alive. Roger Hayward served his father from before Knight had been born and was loyal to a fault, despite his father's flaws.

"My lord, we were not sure whether to expect you." Hayward's expression betrayed no emotion as his gaze flicked coldly over them both, but Knight doubted he was thrilled at his arrival. "There is little ready for your arrival."

Knight nodded. "I will not stay long. Once everything is settled, I shall be leaving."

Hayward gave a curt nod. "As you will, my lord."

"Send word to my father's lawyer if you will. I would meet with him tomorrow to begin settling matters." He offered an arm to Louisa to lead her into the house. She took it, but the look of awe had yet to fade from her expression. "Have one of the guest rooms made ready. Mrs. Carter will need a bath poured. "

"Of course, my lord."

"Is the household able to serve dinner?" Knight questioned.

Hayward's expression faltered a jot. Just enough for Knight to see a hint of annoyance behind the indifference.

"Yes, my lord. We have lost some staff since your father's death but we are quite capable of looking after you and your...friend." Hayward's lips tightened.

"Good." Knight led Louisa into the hallway.

Patterned tiles made their footsteps echo in the vast space. Two marble columns led the gaze up toward a ceiling painted with cherubs and various Greek gods. The room had been re-decorated since the last time he set foot in it, and for that he was somewhat grateful. By the looks of it, the majority of his child-hood memories had been rebuilt or papered over. It would make this whole thing much easier.

Knight released Louisa long enough to remove his hat and shrug out of his jacket before aiding her with hers and handing them off to Hayward. With an infinitesimal bow, the man left them in the empty hallway. Louisa craned her neck to peer at the ceilings.

"Goodness me," she breathed.

"It did not look like this when I lived here."

She eyed him. "You can be quite commanding when you wish to be. *Have one of the guest rooms made ready,*" she mimicked.

Knight grunted. None of this felt natural, and he regretted Louisa having to witness it all. However, he could not help but be grateful for her company. Handling Hayward and whatever else he'd face seemed easier with her at his side.

She paced across the room, her boots echoing in the vast space to study the large painting that hung in the entranceway. He avoided looking at it. That was the one thing that had not changed. As soon as his father had inherited the house, the painting had been commissioned and hung there forever, ensuring all who entered knew that this was the territory of Viscount Marsden.

"He looks like you."

"Without the scars." Knight glanced only once at the painting.

It was true. In his youth, his father had looked almost exactly the same as Knight. What a disappointment it must have been to his father to realize looks were the only thing they shared. His father's selfishness and callousness had failed to pass onto Knight and that frustrated the man to no end.

"Where is everyone?" She came back to his side.

"I imagine some will have left once my father passed. Their future is uncertain so they would have applied for new jobs."

Louisa grimaced. "I know how they feel."

"We will secure your future, Louisa. Once we have returned, Hugh will pay for his deception." He shook his head. "You should have returned with Abigail and you could have resolved the matter more quickly."

"Is my company so terrible?" Her lips curved, but Knight heard the inkling of doubt there.

Not that he knew how to respond. Her company was far from terrible. Torturous, yes. Tempting, indeed. Never terrible, however.

Hayward saved him from responding when he slipped into the room from the door at the rear that was embedded into the wall so as to hide the servant's entrance.

"Your rooms are ready, my lord." The butler did not wait for a response and turned on his heel toward the door at the side of the room.

Knight took Louisa's hand unthinkingly. Her fingers curled around his, a perfect fit. He should have released her then and there but could not bring himself to. So he led her after Hayward until they caught up with him on the grand carved staircase. Once they had worked their way through the long corridor that sliced through the center part of the house into the wings, Hayward stopped and opened a door. "This is the guest room."

Knight ushered Louisa in. Though the air was a little stale, the room was clean and prepared with an empty bath. Knight knew little of fashion, but he had no doubt the oriental fabric on the walls and the overbearing black and gold furnishings were of the latest fashion—designed to impress whoever his father was hosting.

"Your father's room has been made ready too, my lord."

Knight tensed. He knew it was to be expected that he sleep in the master bedroom, but he'd be damned if he'd sleep in the bed his father once had.

"Is there another room that can be used?" Knight asked.

Hayward's brow raised slightly. "If it pleases you, my lord."

"It would." Knight watched Louisa take in the room, running her finger along the tassels that hung from the turquoise bedding. "Will you be well for a while? I'll have your belongings sent up in just a moment."

She nodded. "Do what you need to do, Knight."

What he needed to do was get out of here and never set eyes on it again. His father's presence could be felt everywhere. For many children, such a house would have been magical, but Knight had never felt anything other than suffocated by it. First by the weight of expectation, then by his father and his demands.

Aware of Hayward watching the interaction, Knight turned to the butler, whose expression remained impenetrable. Hayward showed Knight to a room overlooking an ornamental garden that was sunken into the ground. Knight eyed it with a raised brow. Apparently, his father had spent significant money on the grounds since he'd left. The room was a smaller guest room but the bed was decent in size and would do him just fine.

"Will there be anything else, my lord?"

A moment passed, a slight flicker of disdain curving the butler's lips before he crushed it. Knight shoved a hand through his hair. This conversation needed to happen at some point.

Knight faced the butler. "You are aware, Hayward, that I have only returned to settle the debts and get this done." The butler flinched at the word *debts*. "There are arrears, are there not?"

"I would not know, my lord. You would be better off speaking with the estate manager."

The words sounded practiced. Knight fixed him with an unyielding stare. "Is there still an estate manager in place?"

"Well—" Hayward hesitated and looked away. "Mr. Grimes left but a few weeks ago. I am certain he would be willing to discuss matters with you, my lord."

"Hayward, you always knew everything when I was growing up. I doubt that has changed. Tell me...is the estate in debt?"

He gave a curt nod.

"And the debts are great?"

He nodded again, but barely.

Knight rubbed a hand across his jaw. "I expected as much. The house will need to be rented out, any land sold, and I'll see what paintings and furnishings can be sold on."

"Surely there is some other way, my lord."

"I know my father well enough to know that the debts will be great—greater than anything I can pay off." Knight shook his head. "The house must be let."

"But—"

"Without any inherited funds, it's not possible, Hayward."

The butler's hard expression splintered. "I have worked here all my life, my lord. There are many staff. Many tenant farmers. They all need this estate to continue."

"They need this estate to thrive. My father should have thought of that before he disinherited me, but alas, he did not," Knight bit out.

"If you had but stayed," Hayward muttered.

Knight clenched his jaw. "How could I have stayed? My father wanted me gone. He wanted me penniless."

Hayward lifted his chin. "The young man I knew would have fought for the estate, fought to ensure his father accepted him back." He sighed. "I heard the argument, my lord. I know what happened between you, and I know how he treated you."

"Yes, yes, a butler hears all. I bloody well know that." Knight waved a dismissive hand.

"But you were a fine young man with none of your father's frivolousness. You could have stayed and ensured the estate was not torn apart thus."

Knight drew in a long, slow breath. Heat tore through his veins, and he clenched his jaw. He took another breath in a bid to compose himself. He remembered the same heat, the same feeling of unrestraint the night he'd argued with his father and left for good. For once, Knight had been unwilling to take a beating from him, and he was done with excusing his father's spending.

"I'm going to take a walk, I think. Inspect the estate before dinner." Knight did not wait for a response from Hayward. The damned man might have known him all his life and even been considered a friend at some point, but he had no right to question Knight's decisions.

He stormed downstairs and headed out of the door to the rear garden. A vast lawn led out toward another fountain. Closing his eyes briefly, he took the steps down toward the large water feature. He kept going past it until he was far from the house and turned back to eye it.

Damn Hayward. Did he not think Knight had questioned his decision over and over? If he'd stayed, what would have happened? Could he have persuaded his father to change his mind? To change his ways? Could Knight have avoided joining the Army and...and causing irreparable harm to many.

He sank onto the sloped lawns and studied the house as dusk loomed over it. Amber light glowed from one of the rooms—Louisa's room. Hopefully the servants had poured her a bath by now and she was enjoying a soak. God knows, she deserved a little respite after all she'd been through and their long journey.

A smile tugged his lip up at one corner, entirely out of his control. What a woman she was. So damned determined to protect what was hers while he was resolved to rid himself of this place. Every corner of it was haunted with memories though, and few were good. He doubted Louisa could understand that.

Though he had this unpleasant feeling that she understood him far more than she ought to. He rubbed a hand where the aching throb started up in his chest again and frowned to himself. He'd lusted after Louisa for a long time. He was used to that feeling of distraction when she was around, but this...this was new, and he had little idea what to do about it. She might care for him now, but she didn't know him truly. Not really. She didn't know all he'd done. What sort of man he really was.

All he knew was that she deserved better.

Chapter Eighteen

"**O**h."

Louisa turned to find a maid in the doorway to the bedroom. A hand to her chest, Louisa twisted away from the window where she'd been watching Knight pace back and forth. He likely did not realize she had watched him doing the same thing last night too.

"Forgive me, ma'am. I thought you would still be abed." The maid stepped into the room and shut the door behind her.

Louisa frowned at the gown slung over the maid's arm. "I'm used to waking early." And in such a luxurious bed, she had slept solidly, despite worrying about Knight. Since entering the house, he'd adopted a constant look of strain. He'd been quieter than usual during dinner—if that was possible—but he would tell her little.

"The lord sent up a gown. He thought you might like it." She laid the dress over the bed.

Pale green and sumptuous, the gown was unlike anything Louisa had ever worn. It looked to be about her size, if a little tight around the bust. She reached out to stroke the silken fabric then drew her hand back, almost fearful it might scold her if she touched such a thing.

"Whose is this?"

"Lady Julianna's," the petite maid explained. "She left much behind when she...well..." The maid sighed. "The lord mentioned you know her."

"I do."

A smile curved the girl's lips. "Is she well? We heard that her...um...fiancé did not treat her well and that he was punished for his crimes."

"He was indeed. And yes, she is very well. Married now to an excellent man." Louisa could not help but grin.

"I'm so glad." The girl clapped her hands together. "Now, what would you like to do with your hair?"

"Uh..." Louisa lifted her palms.

"Shall I decide for you?"

Louisa nodded gratefully. She usually did whatever was practical. Running an inn rarely called for something glamorous. She sat while the maid—Flora—did her hair then was helped into the dress. Fingering the silk, Louisa eyed her reflection and almost did not recognize herself. Flora cinched it tight, emphasizing Louisa's generous bust.

"I think if you do it any tighter, I shall explode out of it."

Flora laughed. "It is meant to be tight, ma'am. But you are a little more endowed than Lady Julianna."

"Let us leave it as it is now. I fear I will not be able to breathe otherwise." Twisting, she glanced at herself in the mirror once more. Flora had toyed and tugged and pinned until her hair was an elegant posy of curls. She had to admit, she felt more beautiful than she had ever felt in her life, and it was hard to believe Knight had taken the time to ensure she had a beautiful gown that would help her fit in better with her surroundings.

"You are a miracle worker, Flora."

The maid blushed. "You have lovely thick hair, ma'am. It is easy to work with." She gathered up the spare hair pins and paused. "Ma'am, do you know what the viscount intends to do?"

"What do you mean?"

"With the house. Mr. Hayward said he intends to let it out."

Louisa winced. With all that happened with Hugh, there had been little time to discuss what Knight intended. Or she supposed, they'd had time, but Knight had been unwilling.

"I believe he does."

Flora nodded sadly. "I should have tried to find work sooner. I just hoped that he might..." She let her shoulders drop. "Mr. Hayward said that the lord was a good man and he hoped he might wish to take the estate on."

"I think the debts are too great, Flora. But I am certain he shall try to look after you all and ensure your employment."

"I hope so. I have three little brothers at home and they seem to eat everything!" Flora motioned to the pull rope by the bedside. "If you need anything else, just pull on that."

"Thank you, Flora."

Louisa took another minute to admire herself. She would not get used to wearing such finery, but she could not deny it was pleasant pretending to be a fine lady—even if just for a short while. Especially when she considered that it sounded as though Knight had picked it out for her.

Rolling her eyes at her reflection, she turned away and headed downstairs. She paused at the front door. There had to be some other way of accessing the rear of the house and finding Knight, but she was not sure she dare. She'd probably get lost in the maze of corridors and rooms, so she opted to exit out of the main door and head around the side of the house to catch up with him as he paced up and down the neat lawns.

He stilled when he saw her, and his eyes warmed. Her chest tightened.

"You look..." He frowned and seemed to search for words. "You look very fine."

"Thank you," she murmured. "Flora said you picked out this gown."

He tugged at his cravat. "Um, yes."

"You have excellent taste, Knight."

He shrugged and several moments of silence passed between them. He cleared his throat. "Would you like...that is...shall I show you the grounds?"

"Yes, please."

"There are some new additions since I left but the general layout has not changed."

He led her away from the house toward a sizeable pond, lined with stone and scattered with lily pads. They looped around it in silence for a while but it was not uncomfortable. No doubt being here and dealing with his father's death left him needing time to contemplate.

"I should have everything settled by tomorrow, then we can return home."

"So soon?" Louisa asked. "I am surprised you do not want to stay longer."

"There is nothing to stay for. The lawyer has agreed to arrange the renting of the house and settle the debts on my behalf. I shall speak with the tenant farmers and ensure that their tenancies continue under the conditions of the rental. After that, there is little more I can do."

"I think I would find it hard to give up such a home." She paused to peer at the farm land that was separated from the formal lawns by way of a brick wall. "Is all this yours too?"

"Yes."

"It is beautiful. I had no idea that Northumberland was so striking." From the fields, great hills curved upward, flecked with red and tawny brown. They had passed mountains and great rocks with waterfalls carved between them on their way here. Though she loved the sea, it was almost as stunning as Cornwall."

"It reminds me of home," Knight muttered.

"It does a little. Though there is less water." His lips curved when she looked at him. "You think of Cornwall as your home then?"

He paused and nodded slowly. "I was not certain until I came here, but yes, I do."

They followed the length of the brick wall until it snaked back toward the house. A gray bust of a man interrupted their stroll back, and Knight paused in front of it, his lips curled into a smirk.

"Typical of my father," he explained. "His vanity knew no bounds."

Louisa peered at the writing on the plinth then up to the aristocratic features that were so similar to Knight's. However, even in stone, his father's image revealed an arrogance she had never seen in Knight and doubted she ever would. She looked to Knight. He might not realize it, but he was grieving in a way. If only she could help him.

"Has he already been buried?" she pressed.

"Yes." He pointed toward the spires of the church that edged the estate. "It took them a while to try to find me so he was buried in the meantime."

"Would you like to visit his grave together?"

Knight paused. "No."

"But—"

"I said no."

Louisa twined her hands in front of her. She could not fathom what he'd been through with his father and his life after being disinherited, but she understood the need for closure. Surely if he visited the grave, he would find it?

"I really think you should," she said quietly.

He remained silent as they strolled on, following a path that cut through a thatch of trees. He pointed down the path as it forked. "I used to bring Julianna here. She liked to hide behind the trees but could never quite understand that she was not small enough to be hidden behind the trunks." A faint smile crossed his lips.

"I bet you pretended you could not see her, though."

He let out a dry chuckle. "I did."

"You are a good man, Knight. And good men need to visit their father's graves. Even if they do not wish to."

"Damn it, Louisa, must you be so persistent."

"Yes, always." She lifted her chin.

He shook his head and grunted and gestured to the left trail. "This path leads back to the house. I need to finish signing some paperwork."

"And then all will be finalized?"

He nodded. "It will not take long for me to ensure it is all settled." He peered at her. "The estate manager visited me this morning and suggested we turn over some of the land to mining as a way to fund the estate."

"Mining?"

"There's a coal field under some of this land. It is mined not four miles from here, but it would be destructive."

"And profitable, presumably?"

"Indeed." He clasped his hands behind his back.

"If you mined the land, you would not have to let it out? You could stay here?" Her stomach twisted at the thought of him remaining here. Was he trying to decide if that was the better thing to do? Is that why he was speaking of this? The estate was beautiful and luxurious. What man would want to give up such a thing?

"If I mined it, I could fund the house, yes." His gaze latched briefly onto hers. "But it changes nothing. I still intend to let it out and return home."

The tightness in her chest eased. She noted the flicker of warmth in his eyes before his expression shuttered.

"Besides, there is nothing here for me."

The words were said with a hard edge and yet she could not help hear the undertone in them. Did that mean there was something in Cornwall for him? And did he mean her?

Chapter Nineteen

Rain misted on Knight's skin, bringing welcome relief from the heat that seemed to have wrapped itself around him. It melded his shirt to him and dripped from his hair while he took in several breaths of cool night air. He held the lantern aloft and pushed on from the house toward the church.

This was all Louisa's fault. Damned woman. He wasn't grieving for his father. The man did not deserve one jot of his grief. He was glad the man was dead. One less arrogant bastard in the world.

It was too hard to explain that he'd been grieving for someone else his entire life, and that he'd been the cause of his death. He'd hoped to avoid doing this altogether, but Louisa's words would not leave him in peace. Hours of restless sleep filled with hallucinations had left him with little choice—he needed to visit his father's grave.

With quick strides, he cut across the lawns toward the church. Lanterns were lit at the entrance but the small estate church was cloaked in gloom. There were better times to visit a graveyard he supposed, but after his time in battle, there was little about death that scared him.

He stopped under the wood lychgate, on the threshold. Why in God's name was he putting himself through this? With a sigh, he pressed on, knowing Louisa's voice would not be silenced until he did.

Swiping rain from his face, Knight cut through the headstones toward where his ancestors were buried. A substantial mausoleum dominated the space. Knight stopped in front of it and let the glow from the lantern shimmer across its surface. He took several breaths and eyed the crypt. His grandparents and mother were buried here, and he supposed his father had been interred here now. He'd not asked about the funeral but with the time passed between his father's death and his arrival here, he assumed it had been dealt with.

"You would not have wanted me here anyway," Knight muttered.

It was true. His father was incapable of caring for anyone other than himself. His actions with Julianna had proved the years had made no difference to him. He closed his eyes briefly and searched his mind for something, anything. No, he could not bring himself to care.

"Knight."

He whirled, heart drumming against his ribs. Lifting the lantern, he grimaced.

"What are you doing here?"

One hand clasping a silken gown about her shoulders, Louisa wore muddy boots with the hem of a chemise peeking out. He shook his head. Damned fool woman.

"I saw you leave," she said, slightly breathless.

He lifted a brow. "And you thought you would follow me. In your nightwear. In the rain."

"Well, you are also inappropriately dressed for this weather." She narrowed her gaze at the shirt that clung to his skin.

"Go back to the house, Louisa. You will catch a chill."

"As will you." She moved closer and glanced past him. "This is where your father is buried."

"Yes."

"Will you tell me about him?" She held up a hand before he could respond. "And not just that he was a bastard."

Knight pushed a hand through his sodden hair and shook his head. Why was the woman so persistent and why the hell did he feel this inherent need to tell her all?

"You cannot make me feel something for him, Louisa. And I have little idea why you would wish me to."

"I am no learned woman, Knight, but I've seen grief. I know how it can eat at someone." She chuckled. "Let us face it, you are hardly the most joyful of men."

"And you think that is because of my father?"

She hesitated. "Well, yes."

Droplets of rain clung to strands of her hair, highlighted by the lanterns of the church, tugging them down around her face and pasting them to her neck. The rain dancing on her skin gave her a slightly ethereal glow. And the bloody woman would not leave him be and go and get dry until he talked to her, he knew that much.

He took her hand and led her over to the front step of the church, all too aware of the cold touch of her delicate fingers in his still-warm palms. He eased her under the shelter of the door and placed the lantern down on the step. Back resting against the wood door, he peered out at the darkness until outlines of trees and gravestones revealed themselves.

"Hayward said you left home after an argument with your father and never returned."

Knight let his lips curve. Of course Louisa had befriended the servants and loosened their lips. He imagined the return of the disowned son had given the servants quite a lot on which to speak.

"I have already told you my father was a greedy man. To the detriment of the estate. I always knew his debts would ensure the end of my family's legacy."

She nodded. "And you argued about that?"

"Indeed." He glanced at her. "What the servants may not have mentioned was that my father also liked to use his fists." He paused. "Never on Julianna, thank the Lord."

"Oh."

"The last time we argued, it was about his spending...which was nothing new...but he tried to strike me. I hit him back." He snorted. "Needless to say, my father was none too happy that I was finally standing up to him. I was told to leave and never return." He shrugged. "So I did just that."

"Oh, Knight." She put a hand to his arm. "So he hit you regularly? Did Julianna know?"

He shook his head. "No, I made certain of that. The last thing she needed was to live in fear of him. I should have taken her with me or something..." He blew out a breath. "But I hardly knew how I was going to look after myself let alone a girl."

"Julianna is a strong woman. She did just fine on her own."

"Despite me," he muttered. He straightened. "Anyway, I joined the Army and..." His chest tightened, and he forced himself to take a long breath. Why did he even need to tell her the whole sorry story?

"And?"

He glanced at her. Because she was a bloody persistent woman, that's why. And because, somehow, he needed to tell her.

Swallowing down the knot in his throat, he straightened his shoulders and stared out into the darkness. "When I joined, there was another lad—Isaac. Two years younger than me and as scrawny as anything. I had already reached my full height so I watched his back, and believe it or not, he watched mine." He smirked at the memory. "I was still a nobleman with little understanding of the real world. Isaac helped me navigate it."

"I'm glad you had a friend."

Knight grimaced. "I was meant to protect him, Louisa, but..." The words jammed in his throat. He curled a fist at his side.

"It was war, Knight. You cannot protect everyone." She squeezed his arm.

"No, you don't understand." He gritted his teeth as images flashed in front of him. Blood, bodies, Isaac with his chest blown apart. "He did not die because I failed to protect him. He died because I shot him."

He dropped his head back against the church door, his body weakened by the admission. Droplets of rain pattered their staccato beat on the church steps. He could not bear to look at Louisa and see the disappointment in her face, to view the understanding dawn. He was a monster, and there was nothing anyone could do to prove any different. War had eaten him up and spat him out—now all that was left was the shadow of a man who used his experience for nothing more than threats and criminal work.

He waited, breath held, for her to leave. Or to say something. Anything. He jolted when a gentle hand snaked around his waist, followed by another. Louisa flattened herself against him, resting her head against his chest.

Frozen, he let it happen. He could not have fought it if he tried. And then...

Then something strange happened. The stiffness in his limbs eased. His breathing grew relaxed. Her head rose and fell with each of his breaths, and her arms remained entangled around him. To an outsider it would look like perhaps she clung to him for support, but they both knew differently. Her warm, trusting body began to ease the ache burning in his throat.

How much time passed, he could not say, but eventually, and somehow at the perfect moment, she eased her head up to look at him. Knight touched a strand of her damp hair and smoothed it back from her face.

"You are the most beautiful woman." The admission came out low and gravelly but it did not feel hard to say.

She smiled and gave a little shrug.

"You have no idea, Louisa...your strength...your courage. It shines from within."

"You have strength too." She shook her head as he opened his mouth. "I did not mean physical strength. You bore so much as a boy, and I know you protected Julianna as much as you could. Then you went to war and protected others."

"I did not protect..."

She unwrapped an arm and pressed a finger to his lips. "I know enough about war to know friendly fire happens. I struggle to imagine you shot him on purpose."

He shook his head sorrowfully. "The mess of war is indescribable. All noise and dust and blood. I didn't know it was Isaac until it was too late. He ran in front of my line of sight, but I should have...been more aware. Or something, damn it."

"What happened then?"

He frowned. "What do you mean?"

"You left the Army after that, did you not?"

"I was honorably discharged thanks to my injuries." He snorted. "Killed my friend and got an honorable discharge." He motioned to his face. "The same battle that Isaac was killed in was responsible for most of these scars. Not all, but most."

"And did you return to the life of a nobleman?"

He scowled. "No, of course not."

"No, you punished yourself, did you not? You took dangerous work maybe even in the hopes of dying." She pressed a hand to his cheek, and he could not help sink into the warmness of it. "You have paid a great price, Lewis Knight, for the horror of war. None could blame you for what happened, but you are a good man, so you blame yourself."

Knight peered down at her. He could not fathom why she looked at him so—with some strange sort of admiration—but her words somehow seeped in, digging deep into his ugly soul, and he could already feel some of the tension easing, just a fraction.

Maybe, just maybe, if Louisa thought him to be a good man, there was something of a good man still left in him.

"Have you ever told anyone about Isaac?" she asked.

"No."

Her lips tilted. "You should speak of him. Often. It will help." When he frowned, her smile grew. "If you have fine memories of him, is it not your responsibility to tell people of them?"

Unable to argue with that, he nodded. He eyed her shivering form and took her hand. "You will ail if you stay out here much longer."

"I will return with you, if you promise to tell me more of Isaac."

He nodded. "So long as you take a warm bath on your return."

"It's a deal." She clasped his hand and allowed him to lead her to the house.

Once inside, Knight ordered a bath drawn and deposited Louisa at her bedroom door. When he went to leave, she put a hand to his arm. "I should look at your wound."

Any fight he had left in him had long since fled, so he nodded and stepped into the room. With practiced efficiency, he stripped down to his breeches and turned his back to let her tend him.

"It would be easier if you get in the bath," she suggested.

He twisted. "Louisa—"

"Do not argue with me, Knight. You were outside a lot longer than I was."

He knew. He knew exactly what would happen should he strip in front of her and let her bathe him. But he'd be damned if he could fathom a single reasonable argument not to. Following her orders, he stepped out of the rest of his clothes and sank into the soothing warmth, closing his eyes briefly as the water lapped over him. Louisa grabbed a washcloth and urged him to sit so she could run it over his back. He shuddered at her touch and concentrated on continuing to breathe. Perhaps if he let her tend him briefly, he could have this over and done with promptly and leave her to bathe.

Except his hands had other ideas. He clamped his fingers around her arm, stilling her. Her gaze latched onto his. His pulse thudded in his ears when he saw her pupils widen. If he did this, it would be different. He had bared his soul to her and there would be no going back.

He did not much care.

He gave her arm a tug, urging her closer. She made a little noise of surprise as water splashed her dress. Knight looped a hand around her neck and pressed his thumb to her jaw, lifting her face so she could not shy away.

"You are everything to me, Louisa. Everything." The words hurt to say. He hadn't quite known they were true either, until he had said them.

She leaned in and flattened her lips to his. They were cool and fragile beneath his mouth. He cupped the nape of her neck and slid his mouth across hers, finding entrance and tasting the sweet warmth there. He rose, drawing her with him, and, heedless of his nudity, stepped out to flatten her to him.

Her chemise clung to his damp skin, but she did not seem to notice or care. With fumbling fingers, he found the laces at her neck and wrenched them apart until he had enough give to force the garment down her body until she stood skin to skin with him. Cupping her rear, he groaned at the feel of her flesh against his.

"You are still cold," he murmured against her neck.

Before she could reply, he scooped her up and deposited her into the bath.

"Oh!"

Holding her hand, he drew her down into the warmth so she was settled between his thighs. Every inch of him burned with the need to take her, but she deserved to be warm and comfortable first.

Snatching the discarded washcloth, he ran it up and down her body until every part of her was pink and flushed. He draped the cloth over the side of the bath and used his fingers to trace every part of her body, following the curves of her breasts, sweeping over her nipples, and making her arch up from him. He pressed further until he found her center and she gasped. With persistent movements, he brought her to the edge, and she clung to the rim of the bathtub with whitened knuckles while she called his name.

"Knight..." she breathed again once her body had relaxed.

"The water is getting cold." He stood swiftly and flung a cotton towel around his hips before holding one out for her. "You had better get out."

Louisa stood, arms wrapped about herself. Her cheeks were still flushed but uncertainty haunted her gaze. How she did not know what she did to him, he could not fathom. He looped the towel around her and drew her into him.

"You are surprisingly gentle for such a large man," she murmured, running a hand along his muscled arm.

He could escape now. He could give her a tender kiss and leave for his room. Run away. Just like he had been doing his entire adult life. Running from the pain of his past. But for the first time, he did not want that.

"Louisa..." His throat tightened. "I want to take you to bed."

She nodded, biting down on her lower lip. "I want that, too."

"You do not understand, though. I want..." He blew out a frustrated breath. "I want more than that."

A brow lifted, she peered up at him. "You want..." She gestured between the two of them.

He nodded. "I want there to be—"

"An us," she finished for him.

Knight let himself relax for a moment. At least it had been said. Even if she sent him on his way, he had uttered the truth and he was starting to learn that perhaps being silent was not always the best way to live.

A slow smile flickered across her lips. She wound her hands around his neck, thrusting her body up against his. "I think I would like that very much."

He blinked a few times and let the words sink in. Part of him wanted to find the reasons they should not. He hunted his mind for them, but he could not recall what they were. Louisa was perfect for him, and he'd do everything he could to prove himself to her.

"In truth?" he asked when he finally found his voice.

"In truth." She beamed at him and kissed him hard.

Even if there were reasons buried deep, he'd never find them now. He hooked a hand under her legs and lifted her into his arms to carry her over to the bed. Tonight would be the first night he lived without regrets, and he hoped there would be many, many more of them.

Chapter Twenty

Hands clasped in her lap, Louisa peered up at the house while Knight said his farewells. She took a breath and glanced down at her hands, twining them together. A silly smile kept threatening to curve her lips and she had to press them together to prevent herself from looking a fool.

It was foolish really. Nothing was settled fully. After all, they were still just under a week away from returning to Cornwall. Past Hugh's deadline. Not that it mattered. She bunched her hands. Once they had proved him to be a fraud, it would not matter if he had installed himself at the inn or not.

And she could not regret accompanying Knight. Not after what had happened between them. That smile forced its way back onto her lips again so that she was beaming when Knight climbed into the carriage.

A slight knowing smile crossed his own mouth before he shut the door and settled onto the velvet cushion next to her. The smile vanished quickly enough, but he reached over and looped his fingers through her gloved ones. Her heart caught in her throat. How astonishing it was, after all they had done, that a simple touch could cause such a reaction. But, then, him holding her hand meant so much more than him bedding her.

He tapped his knuckles on the roof and the carriage started down the graveled road. Knight kept his gaze fixed ahead on the interior of the vehicle. Louisa eyed his profile.

"Do you have any regrets about leaving here?"

"No."

"You must feel something about it surely?"

He lifted a brow. "Do you wish me to stay?"

She laughed and tightened her grip on his hand. "No. I just want to make sure you are well."

"I am well," he said, his voice gruff. He leaned in and dusted a kiss across her lips. "More well than I have ever been before." He stared ahead again. "Once, I might have done anything I could to save this place, but much time as passed since then. I am ready to move on and return home."

Home. She liked how he said that. He'd talked of how he'd come to feel about Cornwall previously but there was a warm inflection to the word now.

"So, um, we never discussed...that is..." A stuttered laugh escaped her. "I do not even know where you live!" She shook her head. "There is much I do not know about you, Knight."

"You know more than most."

"You do not make this easy." Louisa blew out a breath. "What I am trying to say is where will you live when we return? Will you...um...?"

"Come and live with you?"

She nodded, her cheeks hot.

"If we are to be married, I should think it would be strange if I did not."

Drawing in a long, thick breath, she eyed him. "Married?"

He nodded, his expression unreadable.

"I..." She narrowed her gaze at him. "If that is a marriage proposal, Lewis Knight, you have done a poor job of it."

He chuckled and twisted to face her properly. Loosening his grip on her hand, he swept a hand up to cup her cheek, a thumb brushing her lips. She gulped, her breaths stuttering in her throat as she peered into dark eyes that seemed to dig into her very soul.

"I love you, Louisa." His expression softened. "I have loved you for a long time."

"You have?"

"Indeed." His gaze travelled over her face. "You have no idea the amount of time I spent watching you, wondering what it would be like to claim you as mine." He took her hand and flattened it against his chest so that she could feel the rapid heartbeat there. "Not a day goes by when you do not do this to me."

"Oh."

"I have no flowery words. I only know what you to do me. And that I would do anything for you, Louisa. Anything."

She blinked away the moisture in her eyes. Never before had she heard Knight speak so, and it was almost hard to believe he'd uttered such words to her.

"That was a marriage proposal," he explained, his voice husky.

Grinning, she reached up and cupped his stubbled jaw. "It was an excellent one too."

He frowned. "Does that mean...?"

"Of course, I shall marry you, you big fool. How could I refuse after that?"

His features softened, and he leaned in to press his forehead against hers. She shut her eyes and savored the closeness, forgetting the rock of the carriage and the rattle of the jig and cacophony of horses' hooves. Her world had been turned upside down this month and yet she could not regret it had led her to see Knight for the wonderful man he was.

"As soon as we have dealt with that bastard, we shall wed," he declared, drawing back.

Louisa shook her head to herself with a smile. Gone was the soft, tender man she had come to know, replaced with the fierce warrior, prepared to dole out justice to Hugh.

"Once he knows we have Abigail and she's willing to speak against him, he cannot fight us. He will have to give up his ruse."

Knight nodded. "If he does not go quietly, I will ensure he understands he is not welcome."

"Be careful," Louisa warned, curling a hand around his forearm. "He is still Abigail's husband and father to her children. You mustn't hurt him."

His jaw ticked. "I'd like to do more than hurt him."

"Knight, I mean it."

"They are better off without him. Hell, if she had not run, who knows what his friends would have done to her and the children."

"I'm certain Abigail will not go back to him. But it's not up to us to decide for her what happens with Hugh." She squeezed his arm. "She has the children to think of."

He grunted. "I know bad fathers all too well, and he is one of them."

Louisa leaned her head against his shoulder. "Not all men are like that. I know you would not be."

His arm muscles tensed, and she lifted her head to look at him. Regret made her stomach tighten. She'd never considered she might get the opportunity to have children one day—her life had only ever been about the inn—and yet when she thought of their future together, she imagined it with children involved. Whether Knight would even want them was another thing, however.

Blast, she should not have brought it up so soon.

But if she did not say it now, then when? Once they were wed? No, it was better they discuss it now before either of them made a mistake they regretted.

"That is..." She pressed her lips together. "I always wanted children. Before I took over the inn, that was. Once I married Jack, it was clear it would not happen."

Gaze fixed ahead, Knight's expression revealed little. "I do not know that I am the best man with whom to have children."

"You think because your father was so terrible, you would be too?"

He smirked. "Look at me, Louisa. I have a face that would terrify most children. And a life that is hardly suited to fatherhood."

"That did not stop Red."

"Red is an earl with plenty of privilege, and a handsome face."

"You have a handsome face!" she protested. "But children do not care about such things. Look at how Abigail's little boy took to you. You are nothing like your father."

"I would give you everything you need, Louisa, but children..." He shook his head. "I do not know..."

"Are you going to let your past haunt you forever?"

"This has nothing to do with my past," he said tightly.

"Does it not?" She eyed him until he was forced to look at her.

His expression softened. "Let us talk more on this when we have returned and dealt with Hugh." He pressed a kiss to her forehead that soothed her more than it should have done.

She ran a hand over his cheek and smiled. "You are more charming than you would like to admit."

He twined his fingers back through hers, and Louisa rested her cheek on his shoulder again. They had a long way to go before they even reached home, and she was certain they could figure out everything between them before then. They had both spent a long time living life only for themselves so there would be negotiations to be made, no doubt. It did not stop the warm, giddy feeling bubbling inside her when she considered what their life together would be like, however.

Whatever happened next, she had Knight at her side, and she could not be happier. Now all she had to hope for was that Hugh went quietly.

Chapter Twenty-One

Red stepped up to Knight's carriage with a raised brow. "And here I thought you were intending to rid yourself of all your inherited belongings."

Knight glowered at the earl as he offered a hand to Louisa to aid her down. Redmere House sat a few miles from the village, set into the dip of the valley where the river was once broad and deep. Now the tidal river was not much more than a few feet wide and meandered gently past the grand house. Though larger than his father's—no, his—estate, it had an air of older wealth with less ostentation. Knight much preferred it.

"How else were we to get home?" Knight muttered. "Besides, I shall be sending them back shortly." He motioned to the horses. "Can you stable them for a night or two?"

Red nodded. "Of course." He grinned. "I was not certain you would return. I thought the allure of a fine estate might keep you there."

Knight did not answer and was thankfully saved by Louisa hastening forward after straightening her skirts. "Did Abigail arrive safely? Are they all well?"

Red grinned. "They did indeed. And have been keeping Hannah well-occupied." His eyes crinkled. "For which I am most grateful."

She pressed fingers to her lips. "Oh, I hope they have not been wearing her out."

"Nonsense." Red shook his head. "Hannah has been in dire need of occupation since her confinement. She adores the children."

Knight did not doubt that. The Countess of Redmere was an intelligent and curious woman who tested Red constantly. Something Red needed, in Knight's opinion. Her confinement period was testing them both, however.

"We have done nothing yet, as per your instructions," Red told them as he led them into the house. "But I have word from Drake that this chap has installed himself in the inn, declaring he is your stepson."

Louisa grimaced. "I feared he might. He gave me a deadline to leave and it is well past that now."

"Drake said he had the deeds?" Red asked.

Knight pressed a breath out through his nostrils. He'd be damned if that scoundrel spent a second longer in Louisa's inn. "He stole them."

"Mrs. Stanton explained much of the situation." Red shook his head. "You know you could have let us deal with it, Knight. Nate and I would have scared him away easily enough."

Louisa rolled her eyes. "I would quite like to handle this without bloodshed. I will approach him and let him know that we are aware his story is false. Hopefully he will go quietly."

Red glanced at Knight, who shrugged. He had his doubts the man would go easily, especially if he'd been willing to send his friends to harm Abigail and Louisa to keep the ruse going, but this was Louisa's inn, so he would do it her way.

"Where is—" Louisa's words were cut off when a child dashed out of one of the parlor rooms, his bare feet tapping across the tiles. The boy froze when he spotted them and a grin broke across his face. He stopped in front of Knight and held up both arms.

Knight hesitated, swinging a glance around the room. For some damned reason, the child liked him, and he could not fathom why. Arms still raised, the boy stared up at him until Knight relented, picking him up. The child latched his skinny limbs around Knight's neck while Red eyed him with a raised brow.

"He likes being high up," Knight muttered.

The patter of another pair of feet followed as the other child spilled into the room. An extremely pregnant Hannah followed with Abigail. All of the children were clean, well-clothed, and already less gaunt. With any luck, there was no chance Abigail had changed her mind after being so well looked after.

Hannah embraced Louisa. "I heard that horrible man has taken over your inn. If I were able to, I would go over there right now and demand he leave."

"You damn well would not, woman," Red grumbled. "He's dangerous. Abigail is testament to that."

Hannah peered at Louisa. "Abigail said they tried to hurt you too. Is that...?" She motioned to the bruise still lingering on Louisa's face. "Did they...?"

Louisa waved a dismissive hand. "I am well enough, but Red is right. Hugh is dangerous. If it was not for Knight, I would have been in trouble."

The attractive dark-haired woman smiled at Knight. "Thank goodness you were there then." Her gaze skipped between them and narrowed a little. "Did something—"

"Hannah, why do you not take the children out into the garden," Red interrupted. "I presume you want this matter settled as quickly as possible?"

Louisa nodded.

"Mrs. Gamble can take the baby," Red continued and turned to his wife. "But be certain to take rest should you need it."

Hannah lifted her gaze to the ceiling. "I have rested enough to last me a lifetime." She went onto tiptoes to press a kiss to Red's cheek. "Be careful. And you"—Hannah thrust a finger at knight— "look after him."

Knight inclined his head, unwilling to argue with the countess. Red needed no looking after and could fight with the best of them, despite his privileged upbringing. He doubted Hannah needed to think about her husband fighting while in such a delicate condition, however.

Hannah ushered the children outside with the aid of the housekeeper and one of the maids who took the baby from Abigail's arms. Abigail watched them go, her arms wrapped about herself.

"We need to get this done," Knight said.

Abigail nodded, and her chest rose and fell as she drew in a long breath.

Louisa put a hand to her arm. "I know this must be daunting."

"He is still my husband." Abigail lifted her chin. "But he put the children in danger. I can never forgive him for that."

"Drake will likely already be there. He has been there most days since his return from France to keep an eye on things." Red explained. "And Julianna."

"She is still working there?" Louisa asked.

Red nodded. "Stanton has made few changes, and Julianna wanted to ensure everything was running perfectly for when you returned. Lord knows, she has not relished working under that man." He looked to Knight. "We'll collect Nate and Patience on the way."

Louisa blinked. "Patience is coming?"

"She would hardly let us go without her," Red said, his lips twisted. "If she can be involved in adventure, she will, and she rather fancied threatening someone apparently. Besides, the more of us, the better. Less chance of him trying to cause any trouble."

Louisa opened her mouth then shut it. "I...I...thank you. I did not know everyone—"

Red shook his head. "You have put yourself at risk many a time aiding us."

Knight wasn't certain he could take much more of all this damned emotional drivel. "We had better make haste."

The earl led their group outside and around toward the stables where the carriage awaited them. "I've had them ready to go most of the morning in anticipation of your arrival."

Knight sat opposite Louisa, regretting he could not be nearer her. He suspected Hannah had figured out something had happened between them, though he could not fathom how. Neither of them had given anything away and now was not the time. He still wished he could at least have her nearby. The gap of a mere few feet between them was already too much.

But Abigail needed Louisa more than he did. Her hands trembled as she clasped them in her lap, and she kept her gaze fixed outside while they made the short journey to Nate's country home. Red's brother greeted them from the doorstep, accompanied by his wife, who wore her usual masculine wear. Knight never quite understood how it was the man had charmed Patience, who was not the type to fall for a rake at all, but he'd never seen Nate happier.

"Damn it, Knight, must you take up all the room?" Nate grumbled when he squeezed onto the seat next to him.

Knight ignored him.

"You could always remain at home, Nate," his wife suggested, a smile playing on her lips. "And let the rest of us manage this."

"And miss out on the excitement? Never." Nate's smile dropped when his gaze landed on Abigail. He leaned forward. "I vow he will never touch you or your children again, Mrs. Stanton. You are doing a fine thing. Not many women would have as much courage."

Abigail's tense expression softened. "Thank you," she murmured.

Knight had no idea how Nate did it but the man had such an innate way of charming women. As apprehensive as she was, Abigail already looked more relaxed.

It took mere minutes for the carriage to make it through the village and up the hill to the inn. Knight tried his best to give a reassuring look to Louisa, but she did not seem to register it.

He balled a fist. Whatever happened, he'd get that bastard out of her inn and send him on his way—even if he had to use force. If it were up to him, he'd be using force regardless, but Louisa did not want to upset Abigail any further.

"Ready?" Red asked Abigail once the carriage had drawn to a halt outside the inn.

Abigail nodded, her chin wobbling slightly. Knight remained close to Louisa's side as she drew up her shoulders. Tension riddled her body, and he longed to draw her into him and soothe away her worries. If no one else were around, he would be telling her that he'd do whatever was needed to return the inn to her and have Stanton kicked out on his arse.

He settled for loosening his cuffs and giving Nate a nod. If anything happened, he could rely on Nate and Red to do what must be done.

Inside, the air was thick and musty. Dirt smeared the floor and it was sticky underfoot. He heard Louisa draw in a sharp breath at the state of the place. Usually the taproom was filled with patrons but there was only a lone man sitting by the empty fire. Behind the bar, Julianna glanced up and her husband Drake hastened over.

Drake grimaced. "Julianna has been trying to keep everything running, Louisa. Most people refused to work for him. Sorry about the mess." He looked to Knight. "And I've been making certain he doesn't go near Julianna."

From Drake's dark look, it appeared Stanton had not been behaving any better than his friends at home.

Louisa scanned the room, lips parted. She nodded slowly and lifted her chin. "Where is he?"

Drake thrust a thumb behind him. "He's been drinking most of what you have since he got here."

Knight peered around Drake to eye the man. Chair leaning back against the wall, his feet were atop the table, his eyes closed. Jaw tense, Knight took a step forward, but Louisa thrust an arm out.

"I shall talk to him." She motioned to Abigail. "You can stay here, if you prefer? He only needs to see that we know the truth."

Throat working, Abigail nodded.

Louisa strode over to Stanton and coughed, arms folded across her chest. He didn't stir, so she gave his feet a shove, knocking them from the table and jolting him awake.

"What the bloody—" His scowl vanished and a grin spread across a handsome but stubbled face. "Oh, you are back. Well, you're too late, Mrs. Carter. I gave you ample time and you vanished. The inn is now mine."

"That would be true, if you were indeed my stepson. Which you are not."

"I have the deeds. And the letter," he reminded her.

Aware of his heart beating hard in his chest, Knight concentrated on drawing in deep breaths. All he needed was one thing—one wrong move and he'd be on the bastard in a trice.

Louisa stepped to one side and motioned to Abigail. "We have your wife." She pressed her hands to the table and leaned over him. "I know who you are, Stanton. Your claim will never stand up."

"You can't prove a thing!" He rushed to stand, knocking into the table and sending the glasses on the table clattering. One smashed on the floor, the sound vibrating through the air until it reached Knight.

"Damn it." Knight wasn't standing back any longer. Striding over, he came to Louisa's side and drew her away from the carnage.

Stanton thrust a finger at Knight as Drake, Red, and Nate gathered around him. "This is mine." He slapped a hand across his chest. "Mine. And there's nothing you can do about it. I have the deed. I have letters from Jack Carter. Now get out of my inn."

"I'll testify, Hugh," came a fragile voice.

Knight turned to eye Abigail. She remained by the entrance with Julianna and Patience at her side. With the sunlight highlighting her thin frame, she appeared more vulnerable than ever, but he saw strength in her stance.

"I'll tell them everything you did, Hugh," Abigail declared.

"You bloody well will not." Stanton started toward her, but Knight stepped in front of him. The drink made Stanton reckless, and he tried to shove past him, not even denying who he was. Knight pushed him back, and he landed half on a chair. He righted himself and glared up at Knight.

"What the devil—" He ran his gaze up at him. "Big, ugly bastard, ain't you?"

"Your friends did not fare too well when they tried to keep your secret quiet." Knight kept his voice low and threatening. It took every ounce of self-control to keep his hands off Stanton. If Abigail wasn't here, he'd have taken him to pieces by now. "I will happily give you the same treatment."

Stanton blinked. Several moments passed and his shoulders drooped. "Damn you, woman. Could you not let me have anything good?" He spat in the direction of Abigail.

"I think it is time for him to leave your inn, do you not think, Louisa?" Red asked.

She grinned. "I do indeed."

Red motioned to Knight. "Knight, will you do the honors?"

"Happily." Expression grim, Knight grabbed Stanton by the arm and hauled him toward the door.

He spluttered expletives and fought against Knight's hold while Abigail shrunk away from him, safe in Julianna's arms. His feeble attempts to escape made little difference, so Knight hauled him out of the door and threw him down onto the damp ground, taking a little satisfaction in the thud his body made.

"Thanks to your wife, Mrs. Carter will not be seeing you arrested. You should thank your stars for that." Knight eyed him coldly and leaned over. "If I see you ever again, I will treat you just as your friends treated Louisa. Except there will be no one to save you. And I will take immense pleasure in it."

Stanton hesitated before scrabbling to his feet. Knight recognized the look in his eyes—the desperation that he'd seen in too many dying men's eyes. It usually meant they'd do something rash. Knight braced himself, but Stanton turned on his heel and hobbled up the hill until out of view.

When Knight turned back to the inn, everyone apart from Abigail and Julianna had come outside.

"He will not be back," he assured Louisa.

"You had better claim back your inn," Red suggested.

"And then serve a round of ales." Drake grinned. "I have need of a drink."

Nate shook his head. "You did nothing. Why do you need a drink?"

Drake shrugged. "Watching that blackguard drain half of the supplies was enough to work up a thirst. Besides, I had to keep my wits about me. I've had nothing but coffee for the past week."

"Everyone can have a drink on me," Louisa declared, leading them into the inn. "Then you can all help me clean up."

A groan rippled through the men. Knight paused to mutter to Drake. "Can your drink wait? I have a feeling Stanton will be back."

Drake fixed him with a look. "You will owe me greatly. Want me to follow him?"

Knight nodded. That instinct itched his gut, and one thing he'd learned over the years was to never ignore his instincts.

Chapter Twenty-Two

Louisa shoved her hair from her face and surveyed the slowly improving chaos. Between them all, they had righted the furniture and cleaned up the worst of the mess. She shook her head to herself. Much longer and Hugh would have brought the inn to the point of ruin. Now that everyone except Julianna and Knight had returned home, she took a few moments to stand behind the bar and draw in the sensation of being home.

She'd have to spread the word that Hugh was gone and business would return to normal—all her usual patrons had ceased coming by the sounds of it. She could hardly wait until it was back to how it should be, despite her sore palms and throbbing feet. Her eyes were gritty from the desperate need to sleep after such a long day, but she would not be able to rest until everything was righted.

"All will be back to normal soon." Julianna leaned against the bar in front of her. "Thank goodness. That man was vile."

Louisa nodded. "Thank you for trying to ensure he did not do too much damage."

"It was not fun, believe me." Julianna chuckled. "But I made life difficult for him when I could."

Grinning, Louisa shook her head. "I can well believe it. But should you not be going home? Especially after all the work you have done."

Julianna lifted her shoulders. "Drake said he had to check on something so I was going to wait until he returned, but it is getting late." She scrunched up her nose. "I should have queried him, but I forgot in all the excitement."

"He's probably gone to check on the ship or something." Louisa snatched up two glasses and placed them on the bar. "Which means I think it is time for us to enjoy a drink."

"Do not forget me." Knight stepped in from the hallway that led up to the rooms, ducking to avoid the low beam.

"You have finally managed to get Harry to release you, I see." Louisa smiled at the memory of the little boy clinging to Knight as soon as the children were reunited with Abigail. He'd insisted on being carried everywhere until it had been settled that Abigail and the children would stay at the inn until they could find suitable accommodation. Louisa hoped Abigail would accept a position working with her. It looked like she would need some new help after Hugh had chased off several of her staff.

"The children are sleeping now. Finally." A tiny smile played on Knight's lips that Louisa suspected only she would notice. "She should have stayed with Red. There's much more room there."

"I think you and I both know what it is like to stay somewhere you do not feel you belong." Louisa poured a generous helping of whisky into each glass and shoved one toward Knight.

"You shall have to tell me all about your trip home, Lewis," Julianna said. "How much debt did Father leave you?"

"Enough," Knight muttered.

"I do not think I could have coped with returning." His sister gave a shudder. "I'm glad you have decided to rent it out."

"I didn't have much choice."

Louisa kept her lips pressed together. She doubted Julianna much cared about what happened with the estate, but there would be a few people who would question Knight's decision. After all, how many men would return to a simple life in Cornwall after being offered such an opportunity? She smiled at him, meeting his gaze and seeing the promise there.

Regardless, she was grateful he had opted for that.

"Knight, will you bring some barrels up from the cellar before it gets too late?" Louisa asked. "I want to be ready for tomorrow." She threw back the glass of whiskey and savored the gentle burn as it worked down her throat with a sigh. "Hopefully I shall have customers once again by then."

"Of course." He drained his drink and snatched one of the lanterns from the wall.

Julianna watched him go then faced Louisa. "Why did you accompany him home? You could have returned with Abigail, could you not?" Her smile grew knowing. "Did you two finally—"

A thud and something shattering upstairs made them both freeze. Louisa scowled. "It must have been one of the children." But her fluttering heart told her otherwise. "I shall go see what's happened."

Julianna straightened. "I'll go with you."

"Tell Knight to come and find me." Louisa swallowed. "Just in case."

Julianna nodded. "There's a pistol beneath the counter." She came around and pulled it out. "Drake made me keep it loaded while Hugh was here."

"I am sure it's nothing." Louisa took the pistol nonetheless. She never kept weapons in her establishment, fearing some drunkard might get hold of one. Very rarely did she need to defend herself as it was.

Cradling the weapon, she made her way upstairs. Her breaths were thick and uncomfortable. It was ridiculous. Young children were often clumsy and rambunctious. It was almost certainly one of them having knocked something over.

She tapped her knuckles on the door. The baby was crying and she heard scuffling. "Abigail?" She tried again when there was no response. Keeping the pistol tucked at her side, she pushed open the door and scanned the small room.

"Oh no." The baby laid in the cot, red-faced and bawling. All three children were alone in the room.

"Papa," Harry said, pointing out of the open window.

"Oh no," Louisa repeated and peered out of the window to see two figures hastening away from the inn. The light from the downstairs windows clung to their outlines, and she saw Abigail trying to pull away from Hugh.

Grabbing her skirts, Louisa hastened downstairs only to smack into Drake's chest as he stepped through the doorway that led upstairs. She stumbled back to view his slightly ashen face.

"What—"

"Go look after the children," she commanded, pointing upstairs. "Go, now!"

His wide eyes flicked down to the pistol, but she didn't wait for him to respond. Pushing past him, she barreled out of the door, heart thumping heavily in her chest. When she stumbled outside, she took a moment to search the spot in which she'd seen Hugh and Abigail. She squinted into the night. Icy shards of moonlight rippled across the bay before being hidden behind clouds. Blast, if only it were a lighter night.

Gun cradled to her chest, she ran over to where she'd seen them and stopped to scan the area. The land around the inn was barren, mounds of scrubby grass and rocks scattered the area, but there were few places to conceal a person. What little light the inn provided told her Hugh had not settled on going into hiding.

Drawing a breath in through her tight chest, she peered down the hill but gloom blanketed the area. Clouds had swallowed any remaining moonlight and the lights from the village down the hill dominated the shadowy canvas that was Penshallow. The sea stretched out from the cliffs, an ominous black expanse ready to swallow her if she made the wrong move.

She needed to think. What would Hugh do with Abigail? He clearly had no intention of giving up the inn, and she doubted he'd seized her with any intention of taking her home, so he'd want to rid himself of her as quietly as possible.

Which meant he would not take her to the village.

A salty breeze whirled around her, pressing her skirts to her legs. Bile rose in her throat. He was going to throw her into the sea. It would be the easiest way to rid himself of Abigail.

"Abigail?" she called, as she settled the pistol in one hand, fingers trembling.

She hastened toward the cliff edge and her foot caught on a rock, sending her heart into her throat as she righted herself. The rush of waves beneath reminded her what fate awaited her if she stepped incorrectly. She glanced left and right and called out again.

A muffled scream came from the left. "Abigail?" Louisa followed the faint outline of the cliff edge, more cautiously this time.

Another scream. Then a very male grunt. Her gaze caught on two shadowy figures not far ahead. Louisa rushed forward as a gap in the clouds lit the area and revealed Hugh and Abigail.

"Stop!" she demanded as Hugh fought to control Abigail. She thrust the gun out, fingers shaking on the trigger. Her palms were clammy and damp against the wood, and she had to use her other hand to cradle it.

Hugh whirled around and drew Abigail hard into his chest. "I'll kill her," he threatened, and light glinted off a blade.

He was going to kill her regardless, Louisa had no doubt about that. But she could not shoot him while he had Abigail. Pistols were notoriously inaccurate, and she had no experience using guns.

She forced down the knot in her throat. "I'll shoot you if you do not release her."

"I'll slice her neck first."

Abigail wriggled in his hold but the blade against her neck forced her to still. "Please, Hugh," she begged, her voice clogged. "Think of the children."

"If you had just let this all be I would have sent you money," he spat. "Now shut up." He clamped a hand over her mouth.

Abigail sobbed against the hand while Louisa inched closer. "If you hurt her, I will shoot."

"You can try." She heard the smirk in his voice.

Darkness slipped over the cliff top as clouds flitted across the moon. Louisa cursed under her breath. Now he was but a shadow again and impossible to aim at. What was she going to do?

Chapter Twenty-Three

Sweat made Knight's shirt stick to his back as he hefted up the last barrel and set it at the top of the stairs. Bloody woman could have left all of this until tomorrow but of course she insisted on ensuring the inn was returned to normal with haste. He smiled to himself. Damned, stubborn woman.

"Lewis, come quickly."

He peered at his sister and held the lamp in his hand aloft. "What's happened?"

He didn't wait for Julianna's explanation before hastening past her, through the kitchen and into the taproom. His gut tightened. Surrounded by children—Abigail's children—was Drake. A quick scan of the room told him neither Louisa nor Abigail were present.

"Where is she?" Knight demanded.

Drake grimaced and shrugged. "She told me to look after the children and rushed out. And, Knight..." He heaved out a breath. "Stanton snuck away."

Knight cursed roughly. "Why did you not follow her?"

Drake motioned to the children crowding around him and the squalling baby in his arms.

Before he could follow after Louisa, Drake lifted a hand. "Knight, she had a gun."

Damn, damn, damn. There was only one reason Louisa would race out of here with a gun and the children would be left unattended, and it had to be to do with Stanton. Both women were in danger. Heat flared through him, roaring into his fingertips and making his heart thud heavily in his ears.

"Keep the children safe," he said to Drake, glancing back at his sister. "And Julianna," he added in hushed tones. There was no telling what Stanton might do in his desperation.

Drake did not argue with him for once in his life. He must have apprehended the gravity of the situation, and Knight knew the man would do whatever needed to be done to protect Julianna and the children.

He stepped out into the night, a cool wind sending a chill down his spine and clinging to the sweat on his brow. He took a breath and scanned the gloom. The earlier clouds had thinned, leaving enough moonlight for him to see several feet in front of him. But there was no sign of Louisa or Abigail.

Whatever he did, he could not panic, but he'd be damned if his mind did not race. All his years of fighting and surviving and he'd never once been scared.

He was scared now.

Desperation drove Stanton, and he knew all too well how desperate men behaved.

If he had Abigail and Louisa, he would not head toward the village. At least he hoped not. Or else his decision to head out onto the cliffs was wrong. Falling into a run, Knight followed the faint outline that split the cliffs from the sea.

A crack splintered the air. He froze. No, not a crack. A gunshot.

"Goddamn it." His chest hurt, weighted with dread. She could not be hurt. Not now. Not now she was finally his.

He raced toward the sound and spotted Stanton. Pistol in hand, he loomed over a body.

Louisa.

"Bastard." The word tore from his throat in a desperate cry. It echoed around the hills and Stanton whirled, gun thrust at Knight's chest.

Knight rushed straight into him, sending the gun clattering against rocks. Whether Stanton had loaded it or not, it didn't matter. Knight had no intention of making this easy for him. The image of Louisa's lifeless body sprawled on the ground powered his first punch. Stanton sagged to the ground before he could lift a hand to defend himself. Knight drew a fist back again but a noise from behind stilled his arm.

"Please..." Abigail approached slowly, palms raised.

Breaths heavy, Knight looked back to Stanton's limp form. Blood smeared his face and a matching mark marred Knight's knuckles. He gritted his teeth and pushed his harsh breaths through them before glancing back to Abigail.

Face ash white, her hands trembling, she pointed to Louisa. "Is she...?" She inhaled audibly. "We need to get her help."

Knight unfurled his fist. Christ, he should be looking after her, not trying to kill the bastard. With shaky hands, he crawled over to Louisa. The bloodlust vanished at the sight of her, lids closed, hands unfurled and relaxed at her sides. His throat tightened, and he thrust both hands in his hair while he eyed her lifeless body.

Fingers of horror skipped down his spine as he scooped her up into his arms. He pressed a finger to her neck, but his hands shook so badly he could hardly tell if there was a pulse. Knight surveyed her body. Where had she been shot? He couldn't tell in the dark. Was he too late?

"Did you see it? What happened?" he demanded of Abigail as he rose to his feet and cradled her against his chest.

Abigail shook her head frantically. "She...she told me to run. I didn't see."

"We need to get her help." And he could do nothing out here in the dark. Bile burned the back of his throat. He couldn't even tell if she yet lived.

Abigail followed behind as Knight picked his way rapidly across the cliff toward the inn. He shoved open the door with a foot and strode through the taproom toward the kitchen.

Julianna's eyes widened at the sight of him. "Oh Lord."

"Get the children out of here," Knight commanded.

Behind him, Abigail and Julianna began hustling the children out of the room. Drake pushed open the kitchen door for Knight, and cleared the table, sending everything on it crashing to the floor.

Knight laid her down, aware of hot tears burning the corners of his eyes.

"What happened?" Drake asked.

Knight took a step back, hardly able to voice it. He couldn't lose her. Goddamn it, why had he waited so long to make his feelings known? Why had he been so bloody scared of loving her? He should have fought *for* moments with her, not against them.

"A gunshot," he managed to inch out, his voice strained.

Drake peered at her, his brow creasing. "I see no blood." He pressed fingers to her neck. "She's alive."

Blinking, Knight forced himself to take a true look at her. He frowned and stepped forward. Her chest rose and fell slowly and though her clothes were torn and filthy, there were no bullet holes or bloodstains. However, a welt marred her forehead. Running his hands over her body, he finally allowed himself a long sigh of relief.

"She's alive." A smile crept across his face. The noose of terror loosened itself from around his throat.

Drake lifted a brow. "That is the strangest thing I've ever seen."

"What?"

Drake pointed at him. "Your smile." He peered down at Louisa. "I will check the cold store. See if we have anything we can put on her head. She's going to awaken with a sore head."

Knight nodded, hardly looking at his friend. Her lids fluttered as she fought to tug them open.

"Knight?"

"I'm here." He pressed shaky hands to her face. His vision blurred. A breath released from his lungs and he leaned over her. "God, I thought you were dead."

She winced as she rose from the table and swung her legs over the side. Peering around the room, her eyes widened. "Where's Hugh? What—"

"He won't hurt you again," Knight vowed, his voice gruff. "Louisa—" His voice cracked.

Drake cleared his throat and stepped back toward the door. "I think I had better see...something..."

Knight hardly noticed his friend leave. He cupped Louisa's chin to eye the bruise on her head. "That man has been responsible for too many of your bruises."

"Is Abigail safe?"

Knight nodded. "You saved her."

Her shoulders sagged, and she pressed her forehead against Knight's chest. "Thank goodness. I tried to shoot him when Abigail escaped his hold but I'm a terrible shot. He wrestled the gun from me, but I do not recall much more."

Taking her arms in his hands, he waited until she lifted her gaze to his. "I feared you dead," he admitted. His heart thrust in his chest as he remembered the horror. "I feared I would not get to..." He puffed out a breath. "I love you, Louisa."

She smiled and touched his jaw. "I know."

"No, you do not know." He twisted briefly away, long enough to summon his courage and turn back to her. "I am not practiced with words, but I will try my damnedest to always tell you...I love you more than I thought possible. I want a life with you. If you want children, we'll have children. If you want me to tell you I love you a hundred times a day, I will. Hell, I'll tell you whatever you want to hear, so long as you agree never to scare me like that again."

"I love you as you are, you silly, stern man." Her smile grew and tears shimmered in her eyes. "Though I would not complain about you telling me you love me more often."

"I will try my best," he promised.

Hands to his face, she drew him down for a kiss. He brushed his lips across hers gently but a cough from behind him made him pause. He turned and scowled at Drake.

Drake at least had the decency to look shame-faced. "Um...you need to come into the taproom."

"What is it?" Knight demanded.

Drake jerked his head toward the door. "Just come."

Aiding Louisa down, Knight took her hand and they moved from the kitchen to the main bar. Knight gritted his teeth at the sight of Stanton staggering about the room, blood trickling down his face and staining his shirt.

Julianna and Abigail eyed him from the doorway to the rooms while Abigail's children clung to her legs. The baby slept peacefully in Julianna's arms, unaware of its father's behavior.

Stanton staggered about the room. "Where is she?" He glared at each of them, narrowing his gaze until it fell on Louisa.

"He has to have the hardest head of any man I've ever met," Drake muttered. "I was going to tie him up until we could deal with him but apparently he has already recovered."

Recovered was not quite the word for it. He was vaguely lucid, but his movements were that of a drunkard demanding more drink. Knight had hardly spared the man a thought since Louisa awoke, but he supposed he was going to have to deal with him once and for all now.

"You..." Stanton thrust a finger at Louisa. He went to take a step forward but lurched back several paces instead.

Knight urged Louisa back behind him, but he doubted Stanton had the ability to harm anyone further. This was the last act of a desperate man.

"You ruined my life." Stanton's words were garbled by the blood dripping from his nose. "Everything would have been..." He frowned and swiped a hand across his mouth, swiping a garish crimson streak across his face and shirt sleeve. "Damn you all!" he spluttered.

Knight shared a look with Drake. "Have you heard enough?"

Drake grinned and nodded. "He talks almost as much as you."

Knight ignored the slight and stepped forward to grab Stanton. The man slung a fist at him, which Knight easily caught and pushed back. But the man was slippery and wild, and he wriggled out of Knight's hold, making a crazed dash toward the door.

Abigail moved swiftly, jumping in front of the door and holding out both palms. "You aren't going anywhere, Hugh."

"Damn you, woman." Stanton glared at her. "This is your fault too." He tried to push past her, but Abigail shoved back, sending him sprawling. His feet wrapped around a table leg and he toppled backward, his head bouncing off the floorboards with an audible thud. Groaning, he tried to lift his head then sagged in resignation.

"You did this to yourself, Hugh Stanton," Abigail said firmly as she stood over him.

"I think it's about time we ensured he caused no more grief," Drake suggested.

Knight nodded. "Let's bind him, and we'll give him a ride to the local jail."

"What will happen to him?" Abigail asked.

Knight hesitated. "That depends on you."

"Me?" Her eyes widened.

"I can press charges if you wish me to," Louisa explained. "But only if you wish me to."

Drake nodded. "Add in your charges and he'll likely be sentenced to transportation."

Abigail scanned their faces and glanced down at her husband. Arms folded across her chest, she nodded. "Yes, press charges. I do not want him anywhere near me or the children."

Louisa slipped her hand into Knight's while Drake bound Stanton's hands. "Hurry back," Louisa murmured.

Knight scowled at her. "You should go straight to bed."

She lifted her chin. "Not until you return. You have a lot of *I love yous* to utter first, remember?"

He shook his head. "I am going to regret that."

Drake gave a grunt. "Uh, a little help here." He fought to get the dead-weight that was Stanton to his feet. "Come on, Knight, use that stupidly big body for something useful."

Knight rolled his eyes then gave Louisa a brief kiss. "I will be back. And I will utter anything you wish of me."

Her grin expanded. "I will hold you to that, Knight."

Epilogue

Grimacing as another rolling wave washed up and over his boots, Knight swiped the sea spray from his face. He gripped the slippery barrel with both hands and bunched his muscles while the sand fought his movements, gathering under the container's base. He hauled it up out of the ocean and deposited it with the rest of the haul while Nate dusted off his hands, grinning like a fool. "I wager you'll miss this."

Knight ignored him.

"You'll miss it most," Red said to Nate, unlatching the back of the cart.

Knight cast a gaze over their haul for the night. No, their *last* haul. Drake had just deposited their last smuggled goods, carefully left under the ocean surface for them to collect. It had been one of their better methods of evading the customs men, even if it was the most physically laborious. By now, Drake would be docked and sitting in front of a warm fire. Lucky bastard.

Smirking at himself, he lifted a barrel up onto the cart and the horse gave a snort as though urging him to hurry. Once, he would have relished this. Any chance to put his body to good work and inflict a little pain on it—anything to forget.

Now he was soft. He shook his head at himself. Now he could not wait to return home.

At least this was the last time he'd be doing this. Indeed, it would be the last time he'd partake in smuggling at all, and Louisa was damned happy about it.

He could not complain either. Napoleon had been defeated at Waterloo, the war was over. There was no longer any need for their illicit activities.

Nate paused after hefting a cask onto the cart. "Actually, I am quite looking forward to going back to being a normal, upstanding member of society."

Under the cold light of the stars, Knight caught Red rolling his eyes. Red eyed his brother. "You have never been an upstanding member of society."

"I think many would disagree with you." Nate lifted his chin.

Red chuckled. "I'll ask Patience what she thinks."

Nate's eyes crinkled with mirth. "Ask her. She would only ever support me, her darling husband."

"Patience will have your bollocks for lying," Knight muttered. "Are we to finish this or not?"

"This might be our last job, but I am fairly certain no one died and put you in command." Regardless of his words, Nate set back to stacking the containers on the cart, though he added something about Knight growing bossy in his old age.

"This is *your* last job," pointed out Red. "Knight will be overseeing all of my very legal trading deals. So he is, in effect, in command."

Nate shrugged. "Well, rather you than me. You shall have to oversee Drake and that is a job in itself."

Knight scowled. "Drake will do as I say."

He better anyway. Since both of them had decided to continue working for Red, albeit in a more official way, they had agreed that Knight would take control of the land end of things and also use his lineage—and his appearance—to wrangle some good deals. Drake would continue doing what he did now without the need to slip in and out of France undetected.

Knight allowed himself a little smile. He would not admit it to any of them, but he was looking forward to working without the chance of getting caught. Now their child was born, it was even more necessary he take no risks. The war ending had been timely indeed.

"There it is again." Nate thrust a finger Knight's way.

"There's what?" Red asked.

"That strange smile," Nate explained. "Drake told me it existed, but I had yet to witness it myself."

Red grinned. "He's probably thinking of Louisa."

"I am thinking of an ample quantity of whisky." He lifted the last barrel and shifted it into place, glowering at them both and daring them to argue.

They shared a look, and Nate clapped him on the shoulder while Red secured their cargo. "You can admit it now, Knight. You're as soft-hearted as the rest of us."

"Speak for yourself." Red climbed into the driver's seat and urged the horse forward. Knight and Nate took up position behind the cart, bracing themselves to start pushing. The soft sand and heavy weight of their cargo did not make for easy transportation across the beach, so their additional momentum was needed to get the vehicle across the beach and onto the dirt track leading down to it.

Taking the strain, Knight grunted, his shoulder propped against the wooden slats of the cart.

"I...will...definitely...not miss this," Nate grated out.

Knight had to admit there was little he would miss about the smuggling. While Louisa might be keen to soothe away the aches of their labor, he was looking forward to returning home to her and their son after an honest day's work.

The cart hit the track and he and Nate straightened. They followed Red up the hill toward the old barn they used for storing goods until they were able to sell them on. Nate hauled open the doors, and Red maneuvered the cart in before unlatching the horse.

"At least we've seen no customs men tonight," Nate remarked.

Red nodded. "They've been quiet since the end of the war. I've no doubt they will be back soon enough, though. There are plenty of smugglers still operating in Cornwall."

"With Knight still in residence, none shall dare attempt to bring anything in through Penshallow." Nate nudged him with an elbow. "Is that not right?"

Knight lifted his gaze to the sky and remained silent. His days of throwing around threats were long behind him, especially now he had a son. It didn't mean he would not protect his friends and family if needs be and, in truth, no smugglers would be welcomed in Penshallow, but if he could avoid any such behavior, he damned well would. With any luck, his son Lewis would be able to take up the role of viscount and enjoy the family home if he wished without the taint of anything untoward in his family history. Thankfully his father's debts were being repaid and money was slowly being accrued so that the estate might one day be financially viable again.

For now, however, Knight was more than happy to remain here. Where home truly was.

"Come on then, chaps, shall we get a well-earned drink?" Nate dusted off his hands and shoved a hand through his disheveled hair.

Red arched a brow. "Does Patience not wish for you to return with haste?"

Nate shook his head vigorously. "She is presently enjoying having our marriage bed to herself. I keep ending up sleeping on the floor," he griped.

"She is carrying your child, Nate." Red gave his brother a pat on the back. "This might be your first child, but I thought you were clever enough to know to give your wife whatever she wishes when with child."

"Oh I do indeed." He grinned lasciviously. "But Patience does not have...well...patience. She's ready to get back to riding and shooting. And guess who suffers because of it?" He jabbed a thumb at himself.

"It will not be long," Red assured him. "Then your wife shall be back to giving you hell, just as she should."

"She does do a fine job of it." Nate chuckled. "And I would not have her any other way," he added.

They made their way over the cliff top toward the inn, its glowing lights drawing them in like a siren to the rocks. Knight shivered as a cool breeze wrapped around his damp clothing. He could not wait to be rid of them and curled up next to his wife's warm body.

"Hannan will be wanting another before long," Red muttered. "She somehow forgets what a bore she found pregnancy when she sees your baby, Knight. Of course it does not help Julianna and Drake had a child not long ago either. She is surrounded by babies."

Knight nodded in sympathy. Lewis was only a month old and yet with Patience now expecting and Julianna's child only two months old, Louisa was already speaking of having another. It was hard to fathom that they were all fearless bachelor men not long ago and now all of them were married with children.

The low murmur of conversation greeted them when they entered the inn. A fire lit in the grate filled the taproom with a welcoming warmth that instantly wrapped around Knight. Behind the bar, his sister gave them all a wave. "I shall bring some ale over," she offered.

"Make that whisky," called Drake. "My associates look like they need something warm."

Knight narrowed his gaze at Drake as he approached the table at which he sat. "You could have come and aided us."

Drake smirked and shook his head. "And get these boots wet?" He waggled his feet, which were propped up on the table.

"You should not be buying new boots when you have a wife and child to look after," Knight grumbled.

Shifting his feet down, Drake propped his elbows on the table and raised both brows. "This protective older brother lark is getting tired, Knight. You know full well I provide excellently for Julianna and my daughter."

Knight sank onto a chair and opted to say nothing. Julianna had fallen pregnant shortly before Louisa and he had married, and he had to admit Drake was an excellent father and, despite the fact Julianna insisted on continuing to work at the inn, he was also a good provider. Their smuggling had made both of them wealthy men and would keep them living comfortably for the foreseeable future, especially if they invested cleverly.

Red and Nate sat, both drawing off their jackets to drape over the back of their chairs. Red loosened his collar. "Well, gentleman, that was our last job done." He waited until Julianna had deposited a bottle of whisky and glasses on the table before pouring several fingers for them all and raising a glass. "I think that deserves a toast."

Knight lifted his glass and the others followed suit.

"To you all, for aiding me in this operation that could well have had us all strung up by our necks." Red drained the drink.

Emptying his own glass, Knight put it back on the table. "Neither you nor Nate would have been strung up," he pointed out. "Only Drake and I."

"Well, you are a viscount," Drake reminded him. "So in reality, it would probably only be I who was at any risk." His expression grew smug. "Which I think makes me the bravest of you all."

Nate jerked a thumb toward Knight. "Knight was the face of the operation."

"Well, there is no more risk now. We shall all be legitimate businessmen from now on." Red eyed the bottle of whisky. "I, for one, am looking forward to a little more leisure time."

"We'll see how long you last, brother, before you are begging us to do something dangerous and exciting again." Nate grinned.

Knight glanced at the doorway that led to the guest bedrooms and paused. His lips curved at the sight of his wife, leaning against the entrance, her arms folded. A little disheveled from what was no doubt a busy day, the light from the lanterns behind her cast her fair hair into a halo that made his fingers flex with the need to loosen her hair and see it around her bare shoulders.

"There it is again!" Nate gestured toward Knight.

"Oh." Drake chuckled. "The elusive smile."

Knight fixed them both with a cold state, forcing his lips straight.

"It's well enough, Knight. I think your wife needs you." Red gave him a nudge. "We will have plenty more evenings to drink together, that I vow."

Knight gave Red a curt nod and slid the chair back to stand. Life might be changing for them all but he had no doubt the four of them would still gather at the inn regularly.

Knight paused. "I...thank you, Red," he said, his voice low. "You gave me purpose."

Red waved a dismissive hand. "You did most of the hard work. You gave yourself purpose."

With little intention of groveling, Knight accepted Red's words and ignored Nate and Drake, who were grinning like bloody idiots. Turning, he headed toward his wife, whose smile grew as he approached.

She curled her hands into the lapels of his jacket. "You are quite soaked. I think you should change before you sicken." Her lips quirked.

"Indeed." He curved his hands around her waist and drew her into him. "And now you are damp too."

"I had better change as well, I suppose."

Knight let her lead him upstairs to their room, but he paused outside the adjoining door. "Did he settle well?"

"He is sleeping longer and longer these days, but no doubt he will be awake in a few hours." Louisa smiled. "He is like his father. He needs constant attention."

"That is a lie," he muttered. Knight eased open the door and slipped in, aware of the floor creaking underfoot. Lewis slept peacefully in the gently lit room, his tiny hand bunched beside his head. Knight's heart gave a heavy thud as though reminding him how precious this moment was.

Not that he needed reminding. Having a son had changed him somehow. Made him softer perhaps. It certainly taught him he was capable of more love than he ever thought possible—and he already loved Louisa more than life itself.

He eyed the baby for a few more moments before retreating and closing the door carefully. He turned to find his wife already stripped down to a chemise that skimmed her curves oh so temptingly.

"We should have another," she whispered, opening her arms to him.

Knight didn't need an invitation. He stepped up to her and took her hard against him as need rolled through him. "You have only just had a baby, woman, you need a little rest first."

She gave a little pout that made him want to kiss her into submission. "Do not make me wait long, though."

"I will not," he vowed.

And he was not lying. He could happily have another child, and Louisa had managed pregnancy with all her usual practicality but, somehow, he needed to persuade his wife to rest a little before they embarked on another adventure together. With Louisa having fallen pregnant almost straight after they married, neither of them had scarcely had time to draw breath.

He laid Louisa down on the bed, pausing to push her hair from her face and scan her features. He grinned, and she lifted her fingers to trace his lips.

"You are mightily handsome when you smile, my lord."

He kissed her briefly "My smiles are only for you, my lady." He kissed her again. "Only ever for you."

THE END

About the Author

USA Today bestselling author Samantha Holt lives in a small village in England with her twin girls and a dachshund called Duke. She has been a full-time author since 2012, having gone through several careers including nurse and secretary.

Read more at www.samanthaholtromance.com.

Made in the USA
Columbia, SC
26 January 2020